Love in Little Tree series:
The Wedding Rescue

Runaway Bride

Baby Makes Three

Coming Home

Ghost of a Chance (novella)

Returning Home Romance series
Fixer-Upper

Christmas in Stilton
Santa Dear

Holly & Ivey

Harlequin American Romances:
Marrying the Boss

The Fake Fiancée

The Marriage Solution

Stand-In Mom

HOLLY & IVEY

Christmas in Stilton

Book 2

Megan Kelly

*Elizabeth
So nice to meet you!
Megan Kelly*

To my husband, always,

and

*to my friends who brainstormed this one crazy night in a hotel then later provided feedback--
Carol Carson, Pam Trader and Regan Loyd:
You ladies rock!*
and
*to Lynn Cahoon and Noelle Norris
for your advice and last-minute read-through. THANKS*

Cover by The Killion Group, Inc.
Holly & Ivey: Christmas in Stilton
Copyright © 2012 by Megan Kelly
ISBN-13: 9780988601727

All rights reserved. This book or any portion thereof may not be reproduced or used in any manner whatsoever without the express written permission of the author or publisher except for the use of brief quotations in critical articles or reviews.

This is a work of fiction. Names, places, businesses, characters and incidents are either the product of the author's imagination or are used in a fictitious manner. Any resemblance to actual persons living or dead, actual events or locales is purely coincidental.

CHAPTER ONE

December 21st

Outrage fueled Holly McDonald as she sped to a showdown in the town she'd left at age twelve. Such a strong emotion made for an uncomfortable travel companion. Especially when headed to a wedding. Especially when she was the maid of honor. Especially four days before Christmas.

Little white puffs flew out of the black of the night sky. Wet snowflakes splattered the Toyota Corolla she'd borrowed. Holly turned up the defroster to remove fog from the windshield and cranked the heater to its hottest setting. Between her mission to stop her friend's wedding and the stiff, sideways Illinois wind buffeting the car and trying to push her into the other lane, she couldn't stop shivering. Fortunately, Stilton lay only a few miles ahead. After completing her task, shelter, hot food, and a warm bed topped her priority list. She couldn't think of her own comfort now, though. She had to get to Bree.

A signboard along I-55 for the IVEY CHRISTMAS TREE FARM caught her eye. Her chill abated in the warmth of fond memories.

Luke Ivey. She couldn't honestly say she'd thought of him in years. Once he'd been her closest pal, although they'd lost touch after she'd left Stilton. After his dad passed, he and his brother, Micah, had taken over running the Ivey Orchard, according to Bree.

Poor Bree. Her friend would be devastated when Holly told her what she'd seen a few days before in Chicago, after Bree had left for the holiday at home. From here on out, the Christmas season would always remind Bree of having her heart broken by Alan the Cheater.

Holly replayed Bree's voicemail in her head. She had called Holly's cell Thursday, but Holly didn't have time to retrieve the message until after work.

"Holly, you'll never believe it! I'm getting married!" Bree squealed. *"Alan proposed last night! God, I wish I could see your face! I've been so busy. We were able to convince Reverend Jacobs to squeeze us in on Sunday--*this *Sunday, the 23rd--so we wouldn't have to live in sin. Of course I want you to be my maid of honor. I've picked out a dress for you and arranged for your fitting Saturday morning. Can you believe this?"*

Actually, no, she couldn't. Holly had listened in stunned

silence. It should have been the unlikely speed of the wedding grabbing her attention, but she couldn't get past the part about Alan proposing. On Wednesday.

"I'm heading to his grandma's farm. She's going to let me wear her wedding dress! From, like, 1940. I'm so excited. She's going to adjust it to fit me. Let it out probably and shorten it." Bree laughed ruefully. *"Anyway, Alan said there aren't cell towers close by, so you won't be able to reach me, but I'll be home late Friday night. Can't wait to see you! Bye."*

Not trusting Alan, Holly had called, but Bree's phone went to voicemail. What Holly had to tell her needed to be said in person.

The turnoff ramp for the Ivey Orchard and Christmas Tree Farm appeared between gusts of snow, and Holly impulsively flipped on her turn signal. Someone there liked her. Someone there was easy to be with. And the Iveys used to serve the richest hot chocolate. Even if she couldn't get a hot drink, she could at least warm up in the store. No reason to hurry and tell Bree something that would devastate her, especially as she wouldn't be back until late. Hopefully, Luke would be inside, and they could catch up on the old days. Had her childhood buddy changed? Would they still be able to read each other's minds?

Judging by the crowd in the parking lot, the Christmas tree business proceeded as briskly as the wind gusting through the evergreens. The smell of pine made her nostalgic. Her favorite Christmases had been spent in Stilton. Caroling, bonfires, ice skating and, of course, the Star Night tree lighting in the town square. Originally, her grand plan for this year had been to snuggle up with the novel she'd bought herself as a present. Until Bree's call announcing her surprise wedding on the twenty-third.

Holly hustled inside the shop, rubbing the sleeves on her black wool coat to chase the chill. People huddled around the same two wood stoves she remembered, one of which she delighted to see stood near a counter with the free hot chocolate. She'd have paid for it any time, and on a day like this, the Iveys could be making some serious cash. Eyeing the crowd, she added mini marshmallows to her steaming drink. No one looked familiar. She took a sip and let out an appreciative sigh over the decadent chocolate. Luke and his brother continued to use their mom's recipe. Sheer perfection in a cup.

Senses still tuned to life in the big city, she became aware of a tall man watching her as she drank. His blue eyes reminded her of Luke as a boy, wearing a serious expression as he'd re-assembled something he'd dismantled. This guy's frown and rumpled hair made him appear a little stressed.

He stepped up to her, and she tilted her head back, despite the three inch heels on her black leather boots. Luke or Micah?

While Luke had been her best buddy, his younger brother had been an occasional tagalong companion. This man searched her face, his eyes the deep Ivey blue. His forest green Ivey Orchard vest deepened the hue. But only Luke had that little scar over his eyebrow from when she'd pushed him out of their treehouse.

"Luke?"

Some of the reserve left his face as his posture eased. "I'm sorry for staring. I feel like I should know you."

She smiled wider with delight at seeing him. "I should hope so. You're the only boy I've ever trusted with my binoculars. Which you promptly broke."

His face lit with recognition. "Holly?" At her nod, he swept her into a hug. "Of course. You're home for Alan and Bree's wedding."

"Something like that." Her old friend had developed muscles. She wanted to fan herself. He was hot and making her so.

"This is perfect. Are you doing anything right now?" He snatched away the cup and pitched it into the trash bin behind her.

"Hey! I wanted that last sip."

He grabbed her hand and dragged her along the path he cut through the customers.

"I'm delighted you want to catch up," she said as she teetered along behind him. "But I'll be here all weekend. I just stopped in to say hello. And you have all these customers."

"I know the store's full. That's the problem." The outside door opened as a man entered, and Luke darted through with her in tow. An oversized shed dressed as a small house sat a few yards off to the left.

"I can't believe this timing," he continued. "You're a life saver."

"I am?" Her insides grew as cold as her cheeks. This didn't sound like just catching up. It sounded like Trouble. Being included in Luke's plans had usually ended with her being grounded. "How?"

He pulled open the shed door to reveal a darling living room decked out for the season. He nudged her in where red carpet covered the floor. A large golden throne upholstered in dark green, heavy-weight twill sat in the middle of the room in front of a camera on a tripod.

"Our Mrs. Claus is sick. I need you to fill in."

"What?" She stared as he flipped on lights on the Christmas tree with its icicle ornaments. "Don't you or Micah have another employee or a girlfriend you can hoodwink into this gig?"

Bree had mentioned that Luke hadn't become serious with anyone since his last girlfriend broke up with him. But "not serious" and "not dating" weren't the same thing. And girls had always chased Micah, even in grade school.

"No. I was assessing the crowd for a stand-in when I saw you."

Did that mean he didn't have a girlfriend or his girlfriend wouldn't do it? Not that she cared, other than idle curiosity.

Luke's five o'clock shadow made him too scruffy to pose as anything but a man. As did his height, his broad shoulders, and his general *maleness*. The boy she remembered had grown into a compelling guy. "What about putting a wig on Micah?"

"He's taking pictures." Luke turned. "Why? Are you going somewhere right now?"

"Yes, I'm--"

"Are you *late* going somewhere?" Luke interrupted. "Can you phone and explain to whoever's expecting you? That would be Bree, right?"

Unable to predict when she'd get away from work and certainly not knowing she'd arrive in Stilton around six, Holly hadn't made any firm plans. Bree still hadn't called when Holly had pulled into the parking lot. Not that she would confess her lack of plans to Luke. He'd likely monopolize her all night.

She grinned at the thought before catching herself. This was Luke, after all. Thinking about him romantically was...different. He'd grown into an amazingly handsome man, but underneath remained the boy who knew all her childhood secrets.

"Can't you spare me half an hour or so," he continued,

"*please*, for old time's sake? Didn't you see all those kids?"

She hadn't noticed the kids in particular, but a visit with Santa explained why so many families were out on such a wicked evening.

Of course, he'd have to bring up *for old time's sake.* She couldn't turn him down now, she thought on a sigh. They shared too much history, and too many good memories remained.

She didn't have anywhere to rush to, other than to break her best friend's heart.

"I really need you, Holly. If I had another option, I wouldn't ask."

Her gut clenched at his words. "I guess I could help out for a little bit."

He gave her a one-armed hug this time instead of swinging her around, more like her old friend. "Don't worry. It'll take less than two hours."

"Hold on a minute. How did this become two hours?"

He glanced away, most likely to avoid meeting her eye. She'd only been half-right to describe it as hoodwinking someone into the job. She'd been out-and-out blindsided.

Luke looked at her and smiled. She supposed he meant it to reassure her, but it made her heart race instead.

"It's Star Night," he said. "The ceremony starts at nine, so I'll have to be out of here before then. Micah will finish closing the shop when I leave."

Star Night. Her chest ached with memories. The tree lighting ceremony held a magical, never forgotten place in her heart. Would it hold the same appeal for her as an adult? "Stilton still puts up a huge tree in the town park?"

"It's tradition." His matter-of-fact reply encapsulated the old-fashioned charm of the town.

Her nomadic family hadn't developed many traditions, for the holidays or anything else. They weren't even gathering this year. She'd had no one to share the holiday with before Bree's call.

Christmas in Stilton had always held a special place in Holly's heart. Maybe because she'd been a child or maybe because she'd never lived in a small town after her family left here. Not that Luke needed to know why she'd capitulated. He had ammo enough.

"Okay, fine." Her tone implied he'd dragged her into the act as surely as he'd dragged her out of the shop. Hopefully, he wouldn't hear the tingle of excitement that being Mrs. Claus evoked. "We wouldn't want to spoil tradition."

"You're the best friend ever, Holl. Always have been."

"Yeah," she muttered, thinking of Bree's likely response to her next undertaking. "I may need you to remind people of that later."

"I could always depend on you. I'm glad you haven't changed. Although you do need to *get* changed. I'll show you the outfit."

She glanced around the room set up to receive the children. "Where's Santa?"

His lips twitched into an almost-smile.

She stiffened. "Hey, I'm not doing this alone. No kid wants to visit with Mrs. Claus. They want the big guy."

He bowed from the waist. "Pleased to meet you, Mrs. C. I'm the big guy."

If she'd encountered this man on the street, she would have stolen a second look, but she wouldn't have recognized him. He'd grown taller, more muscular, and, most outstanding of all, more confident. He oozed sex appeal but also came across as a man to cuddle up with while reading a book. Someone to cook dinner for, then go to bed with. Comfortable, but hot.

She gave him the once-over while he straightened the seating. Was she eyeing Luke again? *Luke?* Worse still, he passed inspection with no drool left to spare. Her old friend had been gawky and geeky. This man had her checking her breath for freshness.

Good grief. She couldn't believe she harbored amorous thoughts about Luke. Her Luke. Only...not. Her attraction to him disconcerted her. She might even be blushing. Although he wasn't exactly a stranger, he wasn't her twelve-year-old pal either.

"Here's the changing room." He gestured to a small area

behind a thin red curtain dotted with holly leaves. Reaching in, he pulled out a hanger with a Santa suit. "Space is limited, but I won't look if you don't." His grin reminded her of the old days and brought a jab of sharp joy. "Besides, I've seen it before."

"Not the grown-up version you haven't. I've changed from when we were ten."

He looked her up and down. And back up a second time, making her mouth go dry. "I can see that," he said. "You used to be scrawny."

Her face flaming, she stepped past him and swiped the curtain closed.

She dropped her coat and tugged off her sweater, overly-aware of the noises he made through the thin cotton divider. She banished both the image of him dropping his pants and her urge to peek. "You're one to talk, buddy."

"True. I was a bean pole with rubber limbs. That was my nickname in high school. Beanpole." A grunt sounded, and she pictured him pulling on Santa's boots. "I had no coordination, but fortunately that changed, too."

She swallowed the automatic flirty response she'd have given a man in Chicago. She couldn't flirt with Luke. It was just plain weird that she found him so different and so much the same. And so appealing.

Holly peeled out of her boots and jeans then yanked the dress over her head. She didn't have to worry that she'd attract

Luke. Or anyone. This wasn't a short-and-sexy Mrs. Claus outfit for a corporate Christmas party. The ankle-length, frumpy red velvet dress had sewn-in padding in the bust, torso and rear. The gray wig with its top-knot bun itched as much as the dress. Small square-framed glasses that were almost in style again--but not--perched on her nose. Granny glasses. With a sigh, she pulled on the green felt elf shoes with a bell on the pointed ends. She hoped he looked as ridiculous as she felt.

"Ready?" she called.

Luke couldn't believe his luck. Not only had he found a Mrs. Claus to fill in for pictures with the kids, but it was his best friend from childhood, home for the holidays. Added to that, he'd have the honor of serving as best man when Alan, his closest friend from high school, got married. All in all, the holidays were shaping up to be memorable.

It didn't hurt any that his "old buddy" Holly had grown up to be hot. They'd spend a lot of time together in the next few days preparing for the wedding of her best friend to his. They'd be paired up for the wedding dinner and dancing, which could lead to more, if they had any chemistry of that sort. He grinned. What would it be like to kiss the girl who taught him to gig frogs?

Holly stepped out and forever banished the image of that scrappy tomboy. Luke forgot about his task and just stood staring. Even the padded dress couldn't hide her appeal. The ugly wig hid her rich brown hair with the lighter streaks running through, like caramel swirled through chocolate. Her brown eyes glimmered with laughter behind the old-fashioned lenses. She sparkled. Creamy cheeks rounded down to a soft mouth that confirmed she was no longer ten. Maybe the ideas those red, full lips created in his head made her appear more mature. His mouth went dry, but he had to say something. He cleared his throat. "You'll never convince anyone you're an old woman."

"I'll layer on some face powder. Do you have something to age you when you attach the beard?"

"There's some stage makeup in the box over there. We'll make do."

"Then you might want to finish putting on your pants."

He glanced down at his zipper, glad to discover she was teasing. She crossed to the box while he hitched the wide red suspenders over his shoulders and adjusted the padding. "This stuff stays in place while the kids sit on my lap but it's heavy."

"Here." She extended the beard to him, with some gummy stuff on it to make it stick. "I haven't seen spirit gum since those plays back in high school."

"Where did you wind up going to high school?"

"We lived in Phoenix my freshman year." She pressed the beard to his chin, lapping the sideburns over her hands. "I went to Portland, Oregon, for the next two, then finished my senior year in Boston." Her fingers smoothed the gummy hair up his cheeks, pressing gently but firmly.

A prickle of awareness hit him. Her touch, the warmth of her body so close to his, and her flowery perfume all affected him. Had it not been Holly MacDonald standing before him, he might have pulled her closer. Might have stolen a kiss. Might have tried for more. He swallowed. "What, uh, roles did you play?"

She smiled. "I could never act, as you may remember from the times I flubbed when lying about our shenanigans. But I worked with costumes and loved making props and scenery. Did you ever act?"

"I was never in a school play, but I got out of a speeding ticket once."

She chuckled. "I never could talk myself out of one. Fortunately, I don't own a car now since I don't have to drive often in Chicago."

Luke couldn't imagine not having his truck, but then, he worked outside of town at the Orchard. Their vastly different lifestyles made him sad, but he couldn't pinpoint why. So he changed the subject. "Micah got this face glue from the woman he's dating. What we'd been using didn't stick as firmly as we'd like. Jayne teaches kindergarten, and I guess they do a lot of plays at the elementary school. Her sister who has the flu was supposed to be our Mrs. Claus."

"And Micah's girlfriend couldn't do it because...?"

"She the kindergarten teacher," he repeated.

"Oh, right. The kids would recognize her."

"She's also been taking care of her sister, and now she's starting to feel sick. We didn't want to chance the kids getting the flu."

Holly poked at her wig in the mirror. "And your girlfriend?"

He grinned, taking her off-hand question and the way she avoided his eyes as signs of interest rather than friendly curiosity. Holly being attracted to him made his awareness of her a little less weird. "I'm not dating anyone right now."

She nodded and lined her face with makeup pencils then applied powder. He'd played Santa since his dad passed, but he'd never looked as believable as Holly did. She turned to do him up. He grimaced as she aged his face, making her laugh.

"Stop being such a girl," she said.

"A girl would enjoy make-up." He pushed her hand away. "That's enough. I'm sure I look older than Mrs. Johnson did when we had her."

"We had her my last year here. Sixth grade," she said in a soft tone. "Did she pass on?"

He made a scoffing noise as he pulled on his red jacket and wide black belt. "That woman is too stubborn to even fully retire. She's still substituting. My cousin's kid had her a few weeks ago."

"You're kidding. She must be about one hundred and twenty years old."

The door banged open. "You decent?" Micah stepped in then came to a stop when he spotted Holly. "Well, hello, Mrs. Claus. Sorry, I would have knocked if I'd know Luke found anyone. Or anyone so beautiful."

"It's Holly McDonald," Luke said, cutting off Micah's nonsense. She looked like someone's grandma. His brother would be embarrassed when he realized he'd flirted with their former neighbor.

"Good to see you again, Micah."

"Hey, Holly. Uh, nice of you to step in."

She laughed. Micah clearly had no idea who she was. "Holly from next door. Back when you were nine."

Micah's mouth dropped open before he laughed and hugged Holly up off her feet, swinging her back and forth.

Luke frowned. Micah should knock it off before he cracked her rib.

He set her down, still grinning like a loon while she adjusted the stuffing in her red dress.

"What are you doing in town?" he asked.

"She's here for Alan and Bree's wedding, of course."

"That's right," Micah said. "You and Bree were friends."

"Still are." She glanced at her hands, folded across her middle. "I hope we always will be. Anyway, we arranged to go to the same college. We roomed together without killing each other or ruining our friendship."

"I'd love to catch up while you're here. Save me a dance at the reception, okay? But right now, we've got cranky parents worrying about the weather, and about twenty kids with last minute instructions for Santa."

Luke groaned in a deep Santa voice. "It happens every year. What are the elves going to say when I hand them the new list?"

"Bribe them with cookies. You don't need any more." Holly poked his padded stomach. "There's more than a bowlful of jelly in there."

He tugged on her wig, pulling it askew. "They eat enough of your cookies already, Mrs. Claus."

"Hey, cut it out." She crossed to the mirror and tweaked pieces of hair back inside the gray.

Micah retrieved the camera from the locked cabinet. "As fun as it is watching you two rediscover your old friendship--by acting like twelve-year-olds--we need to get started if we plan to get the kids out of here before the Star Night ceremony."

"Sorry," Holly said. "That was my fault. I knew he'd get me in trouble."

"I'm sure it was hardly ever your fault," Micah said.

Wrong once again, bro. Luke smiled to himself. At least half the time, Holly had planned their more dangerous escapades. "Remember the smoke bomb?"

She laughed. "I'd rather not."

"Is that like 'Remember the Alamo?'" Micah asked. "Luke, sit in the chair while I do a dry run with Holly."

Luke took his seat.

"Better not to ask," Holly said to Micah. "If you don't know, they can't charge you with accessory."

"The smoke bomb?" Micah narrowed his eyes. "The school gym?"

Holly folded her hands, glancing at Luke. "I don't recall."

"Me, neither," Luke said. "And no one can prove anything."

"I'm glad they didn't have cameras in schools back then," Holly said. "We'd have been in so much trouble."

"Delinquents." Micah smiled. "We had to get this camera two days ago and it's a little finicky. It'll be fine. I just need to adjust it."

"Is there anything I can do to help?" she asked.

Luke kept his eye on Holly as Micah showed her what he was doing. They stood really close together, their bent heads almost touching. The shutter clicked a few times.

Micah pointed to the machine in the corner. "Holly, is there any chance you know how to work the printer? Because that's your job. It's pretty simple once you figure out all the buttons."

They moved to the corner where Micah proceeded to walk her through the process. She held up a photo and laughed.

"You're Grumpy Santa." She brought the picture over to Luke. "That'll just scare off the children."

He shrugged, self-conscious about being caught glaring at them. "I don't have to be Jolly Santa until there's a kid in here."

"Hey," Micah said, "while you're right there, Holly, sit on his lap so I can adjust for height. We always get teenage girls posing together."

Micah moved behind the camera again, attention seemingly on the adjustment. But Luke suspected him of foul play. They had teenagers in here every night. Determined for the situation not to be uncomfortable, Luke patted his knee and made it a joke. "Come tell me what you want, little girl."

"Oh, now you're Pervy Santa?" She perched on his leg, holding her weight off him by grasping the back of the chair.

The shutter clicked.

"Let's try that again," Micah said. "It's out of focus for some reason. Is one of you moving?"

"You don't weigh anything," Luke told her as the shutter clicked again and again. "Relax. You're making the picture blurry."

"I am not." But she released her death grip on the chair and put her hand on his shoulder.

"I was wrong," he panted out, as though in agony, "you weigh a ton."

She laughed. "Your fault."

"You've been sneaking my cookies, Mrs. C."

"I take the Fifth."

"Five cookies at a time? I believe it."

"Don't make me blacken your eye, Santa. I can do it, too."

"I remember."

Micah straightened. "Okay, you two. I've got it."

Holly jumped off his lap as though sitting on fire ants.

"You did great, Holly. Santa's not grumpy anymore." Micah smirked. "Just the opposite, I'd say."

Luke scowled at his brother. Best to change the subject and smooth over the sudden awkward tension in the room. At least, *he* felt it, so surely Holly did, as well. "Here's the deal. Any child can visit with Santa for free. Teens and adults pay four dollars just to visit with Santa, one dollar of which we donate to the county food pantry. Parents can take pictures if they want, but the instant print photos we take cost three dollars. Teens and adults wanting a picture pay another dollar."

She tipped her head, considering. "I imagine the teens take pictures with their phones, so you're netting three bucks off them. That would help defray the paper and ink costs for the little kids' photos. Are you breaking even?"

Luke spied the red velvet hat with its white ball and trim and retrieved it from the shelf. "Barely, but we have our reasons for doing it this way. One, it's Christmas. Two, having Santa's Cabin brings more customers out here. Even if they don't buy a tree, they usually get some garland or a poinsettia, cider or an ornament. Three, it creates good will that carries over for the orchard business. We're usually featured in the paper, so we get free advertising, too."

"Reason four," Micah put in, "three dollars seems cheap for an instant photo. Parents are more likely to buy one than if it cost more. We let parents take their own pictures so even the folks that can't afford to pay can have photos of their kids with Santa. So, five, that small amount covers our cost."

"When did you start this?"

Luke met his brother's eye for a moment. "Two years before Dad died. He'd always wanted to do something more for the community than give fruit to the food pantry. He made a great Santa."

"I think it's sweet. My colleagues would have a field day trying to convince you to charge more so you don't go broke."

Micah grinned. "Sassy as ever. And on that note, it's time to open the doors. Are you ready?"

"No," Holly said.

"No," Luke said.

"Great. Let's get started."

CHAPTER TWO

"Are you really Santa?" A boy of about five yanked on Santa's beard.

Holly gasped, Luke's hand flew to his cheek, patting the "sore" spot and surreptitiously resticking his beard.

"Ow." Luke scowled at the now round-eyed boy, then he chuckled. "Don't worry. I won't put you on the naughty list. Nothing wrong with being curious. Now, what do you want me to bring you, Jason?"

The boy's mouth dropped open. "How did you know my name?"

Holly wondered that herself. Luke knew quite a few of the townspeople, of course, but she'd been surprised he knew the name of every kid coming into Santa's Cabin. She didn't believe in Christmas magic, and yet...

"Do you still doubt me?" Santa Luke asked.

Carroty hair flew as the boy shook his head. "No, Santa. You're real. I believe in you."

Santa hugged him. "I know you do. Now, you keep doing what your parents tell you, be a good boy, and you'll get your wish. What is it?"

As the boy whispered to Santa, Holly marveled at Luke's patience and good humor. He'd been her best friend for a reason and not only because they'd been neighbors. The man Luke had become was a credit to the boy he'd been. It warmed her heart to see his promise fulfilled.

"Hey, there, Tyler," Santa Luke greeted a blond boy of about six or seven.

"Hi, Santa." He jumped onto Santa's lap.

Luke grunted and his knuckles turned white on the arm of the chair.

"Tyler Carrow," a woman, obviously his mother, cautioned from her place beside the camera. "Go easy on Santa."

Holly bit her lip. Santa needed protective gear. A white chain mail beard for all those head-butts, armor to keep little feet and knees from gouging his thighs, and definitely a steel-plated cup.

"Sorry, Mom. Sorry, Santa."

"That's okay. No harm done. Don't worry. I'll still bring you presents."

The boy nodded. "Yeah, I know."

"Don't be rude," his mom admonished.

"I'm not, Mom. Santa always brings me presents because I know he's real, and I'm always good. Well..." He tipped his head. "As good as I can be."

Luke patted the child's back. "I don't expect perfection, Ty. Now, what do you want this year?"

"I want Mom and Dad to get us a new house like they've been saying they would. I don't want to have to share my room with the new baby for too long. I want a soft toy for my baby sister or brother, but I don't know which kind we're getting." He eyed Santa. "Do you know?"

Luke grinned, and his eyes sparkled with laughter. "I can't tell you."

Tyler sighed. "I figured it was a secret. So the toy should be something a baby girl or boy could play with, like a rabbit. Only no small parts."

His parents had clearly discussed this with him already, preparing for the changes in their lives.

"Got it," Luke said. "You know babies can't play at first, right?"

"Oh, yeah. Dad told me. Babies have to work at growing so they can do more than just cry and sleep." Tyler wiggled close and whispered in a loud little boy whisper, "And I wanted to thank you for my new dad. He's the best."

The woman sniffed and wiped at her eyes. Holly wished she had a camera to take her picture, but theirs sat affixed to the tripod.

The woman leaned over to Holly. "His birth father died when he was a baby. My husband--" She smoothed her coat over her bulging belly. "Adopted Tyler last year and loves him like his own. It's been almost seamless, except for my mother-in-law."

"The new one or the old one?" Holly covered her mouth, horrified. She couldn't believe she'd asked that, but before she could retract the question, the woman laughed.

"Both, now that you mention it. Sam's mom is distant, but my first husband's mother is a piece of work."

When the boy climbed down, his mother handed him money which he put in the kettle for extra donations to the food pantry. She waved at Luke. "Bye, Santa, and thank you."

"Always a pleasure to see you, Trish. You bring that little one in next year. Tyler can help me figure out what the baby wants."

"Will do."

Throughout the next hour, other children challenged Santa's credibility, but Luke had snappy answers for all the doubters. The children asked for improbable gifts such as snakes, dinosaurs or an entire toy store. Holly had as much fun watching the parents as she did watching the kids and Luke. Some children worried they wouldn't get anything. Through it all, Luke parried, reassured and entertained. Hearts were won over, and Holly couldn't say hers remained untouched. Even if she hadn't known him, she would have been drawn to the man in Santa's chair.

When she tore her gaze from Luke, Holly chatted up parents and children, took money and printed out digital photos. She had such light-hearted fun, she didn't notice time passing. She pushed aside thoughts of Bree and the ordeal ahead. Never had she been so glad to be roped into something by Luke.

Santa's Cabin closed at 7:30 so Luke could get to the Christmas tree ceremony downtown. They cleaned off their makeup and his facial hair side by side in front of a tiny mirror. Holly wore a towel as a cape, not wanting to stain the dress. Luke shed his jacket and padding and stood beside her in a white tee shirt and his Santa pants. She helped remove remnants of his beard glue while peeking at the muscles in his arms and chest. He had a build like a lumberjack. His broad chest tapered down to taut abs, outlined as the tee stuck to his hot skin.

She cleared her throat as she finished cleaning off his face, exposing a five o'clock shadow that she wanted to caress. Jeez, she had to stop *noticing* him. "That was fun."

"You were great. Thanks for helping." He flipped his suspenders over his shoulders. "I have to get changed. I'm going up in the bucket with the chosen kid this year."

"Right." Holly snapped out of her lustful reverie and slipped behind the thin cloth screen once again. She shed the hot, lumpy dress with alacrity and pulled on her layers of clothing.

It didn't surprise her Luke would not only donate the tree but volunteer to help out. Some lucky kid would wave the "magic" wand and proclaim that the star should shine Christmas blessings down on the town. Below, a switch would be covertly flipped, the star and some extra tree lights would shine, and the last weekend before Christmas would officially start.

"Ready?" she called.

"Come on out."

She emerged with her boots in hand. Luke had finished changing already, his hair a bit tousled. Jumping onto Santa's throne, she yanked on the first boot.

"Look up," he said.

She heard the camera click before she registered Luke behind the tripod. She scowled. "That's not fun--" The camera clicked again, capturing her expression. "Luke, stop it."

Click.

"At least take a half-decent one." She finished with the other boot then sat back and smiled. He obligingly took the shot.

"I liked the scowling one better," he said. "More like I remember you."

"Gee, thanks." She rose, disgruntled.

"You were always on a mission, always busy with some scheme. Seldom satisfied with the status quo."

Holly frowned, not thrilled to be remembered in such an unattractive way. Her memories of the past didn't match either. "Why do you say that? I wasn't unhappy."

"No, you were just determined to make everything better. Shinier. Run smoother." He shrugged. "I admired the way you dissected things, looking for flaws you could fix."

"Oh." Was that any better? She sounded like a critical child.

"As a budding scientist, I felt the same."

Well, in that case...

"I took everything apart to see why it worked. Remember how mad your dad was when I disassembled his radio right before the Rams were in the Super Bowl?"

She laughed. "Steaming. He'd planned to take the radio with him to work since he couldn't have his computer on. He bought another radio and I got to keep the old one once you fixed it, so it was a win-win."

"And a win for the Rams against the Titans." Luke looked at the ground. "But a loss for me. Two months later you moved away."

Her jaw dropped. "They're not related events. You know that, right?"

He nodded. "But I didn't at the time. I was miserable."

"Oh, Luke." She put her hand on his forearm, seeking comfort from those memories as much as comforting him. "We didn't move because you busted dad's radio. Why didn't you tell me you thought that?"

His gaze met hers. "When you already believe something, you don't need confirmation, and when you're a pre-teen boy, you don't want to dwell on the crap you pulled. I felt guilty you were leaving. I thought you'd be mad at me."

"I wasn't mad. I was heart-broken that my dad took a transfer."

"Me, too."

A tentative smile crept from her heart to her face, blooming as Luke responded.

He cleared his throat. "We should get going."

Holly pulled out her thin cotton gloves, wishing for something thicker. They snuck out, making sure no children lingered with their parents in the store. After all that work, they didn't want to blow Luke's cover.

"Can you give me a ride?" Luke asked suddenly. "I'll never find a parking place and if I'm any later, they'll replace me. Micah will close up and come later. He can take me home in his truck."

"Sure." They traversed the now almost empty parking lot to her car. The snow had stopped while they were inside the Cabin. Although still cold, the wind had died to an occasional gust, making the night bearable. "Good weather for Star Night."

"I was worried about that snow earlier. I'd hate for Cloverdale to have one up on us."

"Cloverdale has a Star Night now?" The neighboring community had always competed with Stilton. Their kids attended Stilton schools. Their citizens shopped in Stilton grocery stores, as they didn't have any. Their readers paid taxes to the Stilton Public Library.

"Cloverdale tried to copy the star ceremony a few years ago, but no one went. Then they tried to get us to alternate years with them, but the Stilton town leaders refused." He shrugged. "So Cloverdale started an indoor ceremony at the Senior Center. Ours is better, but with the snow and wind earlier, people might have decided to go there."

"Would the mayor call off the lighting?" She thumbed the lock on the remote, and the Corolla's lights flashed under the thin cover of snow.

Luke shrugged. "Haven't had to cancel one yet. But sometimes the name drawn is of an older child, just to keep the kid from having to reach too far over the bucket if it's windy."

Surprise stopped Holly's feet. "Are you saying the drawing is rigged?"

"Not usually. Only twice that I know of. The person collecting names sort of held on to a slip instead of dropping it in."

She shook her head, disillusioned. It shouldn't upset her. Magic didn't exist. A man always hid behind the curtain, pulling levers. She'd just thought because this was Stilton, things were...still pure. Still honest.

"I'll clean your windshield," Luke said into the silence.

"Thanks." Holly retrieved the scraper from the floor of the back seat then climbed behind the wheel. She turned on the car to start up the heater and defroster. The wipers removed the majority of the snow from the front windshield while Luke made quick work of the back. He came around and swiped the top and edges of the front. Through it all, she watched his face, this man who she knew well and didn't know at all.

She could admit it, at least to herself. This Luke intrigued her. This Luke made her think of breathless kisses. This Luke melted her heart.

Would it be wrong to have a fling while she visited her hometown? She laughed. It certainly couldn't be called sudden. She'd met Luke over twenty years ago when her family moved in next door to his. They'd been five and had become inseparable. An attraction between them felt long overdue.

Would they have dated if she hadn't moved? Would their friendship have withstood the awkwardness of puberty or the angst of high school? She wanted to believe it would have. Seeing him now--tall, dark and handsome--made her stomach flutter as though she'd swallowed the partridge out of the pear tree. And the three French hens, as well.

Luke swung himself into the passenger seat and tossed the scraper into the back. He rubbed his hands together. "It's colder than I thought."

"I didn't notice you weren't wearing gloves. How are you going to make it through Star Night without losing a finger?"

"I'll borrow some."

Without thinking, Holly took his hands between hers and rubbed vigorously. But he wasn't a boy any longer. Their gazes caught, just like earlier when she'd been on his lap. Just like then, a rush of heat ran over her. But this time, she didn't care if he knew it. She leaned toward him, pulling on his hands to bring him nearer. She watched his eyes to read his expression, alert for hesitancy, hoping for eagerness. In the faint light from the Orchard's shop, she couldn't decipher his look. He leaned in.

Their lips met. It should have been awkward, Holly thought, in some tiny, distracted part of her brain, way in the back where she could still think rationally. Kissing her friend, her playmate, her cohort in all things Trouble. But when his slightly chilled mouth touched hers, retreated, returned, the tingles racing along her skin were born of excitement, not embarrassment. Her gaze stayed on his, neither one closing their eyes, which made it more exciting. More *theirs*. To see him, to see *Luke*. Kissing Luke. Feeling his lips warming against hers. He drew back, not much more than a few inches, and gulped in air, struggling for his next breath, much like she did.

For such a brief kiss, it packed a wallop. Their entire relationship changed from innocent friends to...something adult. Something with possibilities.

"Thanks for cleaning the windows," she said just to break the silence.

"Is that why you kissed me, as a thank you?" Humor laced his words. "Can I put air in your tires? Pump your gas?"

She smiled.

"What do I get if I overhaul your engine?"

Holly shoved his hands away and sat back in her seat. "Idiot."

He grinned. "I need to take off my jacket."

She examined his thick, dark red corduroy barn coat. The heater didn't work that efficiently. She'd barely shaken off her chill before he kissed her. Then she'd warmed up. Fast. "Is it too hot in here for you already?"

"Absolutely." His voice held a teasing leer. "But I was thinking, you rubbed my hands when they were cold. If I take off my coat..."

She let out a laugh and put the car in gear. "If you take off your coat, you'll catch cold. In which case, I'll take you to the doctor, but I won't take you home with me."

His eyebrows rose. "You plan to take me home with you?"

Crap. She looked out her side window, as though for traffic in the nearly empty lot, trying to hide her embarrassment. Did he want this? Was she moving too quickly? Would a little romance destroy the memories of their friendship?

She took a breath. "How about dinner fir--instead? I'm starving. Do you have plans for after the star lighting?"

"I do now."

CHAPTER THREE

Holly found a spot to stand on the edge of the crowd where she could see the tree's top. She blew on her cup of hot chocolate from the Boy Scouts' booth as Jeff, a delighted boy of about seven, stepped into the cherry picker and waved to the crowd applauding him. Luke handed Jeff the "magic" wand with a bow that made the crowd cheer. Cameras flashed to ensure the child had memories of this moment forever. The bucket rose from the fire engine, and the boy's laughter could be heard from below. Luke's fellow volunteer firefighters maneuvered them into place. Holly's stomach clenched with both fear for Luke and excitement to experience the lighting again.

 A drumroll sounded then a hush fell across the town. Spotlights shot on, illuminating the bucket for the news cameras and spectators below. The streets had been blocked off so no traffic moved. Considering all the citizens in Stilton and probably the four surrounding towns stood around the forty-five foot evergreen in the park, finding a moving car to make noise would have been quite a feat.

Goosebumps raced along her skin. She wished she could attribute them to the cold, but it was the ceremony sneaking under her defenses. Even though she knew how it worked, the lighting thrilled her. The Stilton tree didn't stand as tall as the one in Rockefeller Center in New York City, fewer people attended, and fewer still would watch the event on the local news. But to Holly, this moment represented the wonder of the season.

Jeff cleared his throat and spoke into the microphone. "The lighting of this holiday star..." The boy paused as Luke whispered his lines to him. "Brings Christmas blessings...to shine down on the town of Stilton...and Cloverdale, and all the neighboring cities...and on our visitors. Merry Christmas and happy holidays to all." Jeff swung the wand as though shaking something sticky off of the end.

The star atop the Christmas tree lit then magic sparkles trickled down from it and caught on branches. A strand of lights along the trunk shone in progression from top to bottom. Enchanting, dreamlike, a fantasy.

Holly hugged herself tight as a shiver of foolishness spread over her before she applauded with everyone else. Of course, she *knew* it wasn't magic. Magic didn't exist. One of the firefighters had flipped on those lights, pre-set to sparkle individually. Sleight of hand, illusion, trickery.

Not that Jeff doubted the magic, judging by his flushed

cheeks and wide smile as he waved to the crowd while the bucket lowered. Luke handed him out to his parents and more cameras flashed. She'd have to see if she could buy a print from the newspaper office. This moment, with the man and the boy, held its own charm.

Luke shed his fireman's coat and helmet, handing them to another firefighter. Since he shook hands with many of the people he passed, it took him quite a few minutes to reach her. She checked her phone again. No calls yet.

"It was windy up there, but we got it done."

She extended the Styrofoam cup to him. "It's still warm, but it's not nearly as good as your mom's recipe."

He took the cup from her hand. "Thanks."

"I drank from this side." She pointed to the lipstick on the rim, not wanting it to transfer to him.

He caught her gaze and turned the cup to place his lips exactly where hers had been. A shiver of awareness ran over her skin as he sipped, gaze on hers, unblinking, drawing out the moment.

"Very sweet," he said.

She swallowed past the lump in her throat.

"The Styrofoam's kind of nasty tasting, though."

Did he mean that as an opening, or was she reading more into his statement because of her attraction to him? She'd never been uncomfortable with Luke Ivey and didn't want to feel awkward now. She had to know.

"Then let's get rid of the cup." Holly pushed his hand to the side. Using his chest for balance, she rose and kissed him. She blinked her eyes rapidly, letting him make it a joke if he wanted. "Sweet enough for you?"

"I could get used to it."

She turned and began strolling. He could have been kidding her in return or he could have been flirting. She wanted to growl her frustration at not knowing but settled for clenching her fists in her pockets. They had all weekend to test the waters. If she could find some patience.

"Let's go to the Dew Drop and grab a bite, okay?" He pointed up the street to where a green neon light asked people to "Please Dew Drop In."

"Dinner sounds good. Is it owned by anyone I'd know?"

"No, they're from Arkansas. Opened the Dew Drop a few years ago, serving typical diner fare. We had a French restaurant in that space before them. It tanked, not surprisingly."

"I like diner food."

"You can take the girl out of Stilton..." Luke said.

She laughed. She'd been out of Stilton for more than half her life now, yet memories of the town coursed through her marrow. "Just call me a country girl at heart."

He eyed her outfit from her black wool coat to this season's fashionable black leather boots. "You hide it well."

Holly shrugged, choosing to ignore his mocking. "Since we moved almost every year, I developed the ability to blend in. Now blending in isn't as important."

He walked without answering for a few strides. "Did the ceremony live up to your expectations?"

"Jeff was thrilled."

Luke stopped her with a hand on her arm. "You weren't?"

She shrugged, not wanting him to know how deeply the simple ceremony affected her. "It was what I remembered. I enjoyed seeing you up there. Do you always do the bucket part?"

"Nope." They separated around a family going the opposite direction and then came back together. "We draw names at the firehouse."

"Did someone hold on to your name slip so you'd be chosen?"

He grimaced, his grip on her elbow tightening for a second. "I shouldn't have told you. It doesn't happen often, just when a child needs an extra boost. Such as, if there's a death in their family or someone is terminal--especially if the child is ill. I don't see the problem."

"I'm sorry." She shook her head. He didn't consider it crooked to rig the selection process. How much had her old friend changed? "I'm silly to be disappointed. It's good to make a holiday special for a disadvantaged child."

"It cheers up the entire family, Holly, which in turn cheers up the entire community. That's the point of blessing the town. We all take comfort from it."

"I remember, but waiting to be picked was a nightmare. Each year, I thought it could be me. I so badly wanted to go up there and light the tree, bless the town and start Christmas weekend."

"I know you did. You always dressed like a princess on Star Night, waiting for your name to be chosen."

"You remember that?"

"I remember a lot of things."

He didn't elaborate, and this wasn't the time to ask. She didn't want to read more into it than he meant.

She heard her name called and spun around with reluctance, identifying the voice. Reality intruded as Bree's mother approached. At least Bree wasn't with her.

"Mrs. Kennedy, I didn't expect to see you." Holly hugged the woman who had always held a special place in her heart. Throughout their college years, Holly had received presents and food right along with Bree, as though both girls were Kennedy daughters. Her own parents hadn't sent food or little gifts as often, and only half the time did they think to include something for Bree.

Anne Kennedy's dark hair sported a shiny poinsettia clip.

She'd pinned a silver wreath on her red wool pea coat. The vibrant color made her complexion luminous, or maybe that was her mother-of-the-bride glow.

"Nice to see you, Anne," Luke greeted the older woman.

"You did a fine job with the star lighting," she told him.

"Thanks."

"You look great," Holly said, "especially considering the week you've probably had, as well as preparing for Christmas. How are you holding up?"

"It's been more fun than I imagined it could be," Mrs. Kennedy said. "I thought I'd faint when Alan insisted the wedding had to be this week, but all the plans are coming off smoothly. There's not a lot of time for adding expensive extras or worrying about perfection."

When she trailed off, Holly laid her hand on the other woman's arm. "What aren't you saying?"

"It's happening so fast." Mrs. Kennedy gave a half-laugh. "That's a blessing in many ways. None of the worry and fuss. But, well, there's none of the worry and fuss. I imagined my daughter's wedding as a long, well-thought-out affair with lots of planning and together time. I even bought a bottle of wine for tonight so the two of us could spend some time together."

"Is that the plan?" Holly hated to interfere with their supposed last night together, but maybe her mom--and the wine--would help Bree through it.

"Not anymore," Mrs. Kennedy said. "I forgot to tell Bree I wanted to do this, and she went straight from Alan's grandma's to her cousin's house." She covered her mouth, eyes wide. "Oh, dear, Holly, did she know you were coming in tonight? I swear I don't know what's gotten into that girl."

"It's okay. I told her I'd be late. I left Chicago early enough to miss traffic, but I haven't been able to get her on the phone." Might as well bite the bullet. "So is Bree home now? I haven't heard from her, so I thought she was still out of cell range."

"She's still helping her cousin, Marie, put together the table decorations. She's going to stay in Springfield overnight."

Holly tried not to slump as relief hit her. *A reprieve!* She wouldn't have to break Bree's heart tonight. Although she felt a coward for postponing the dreaded task, she wouldn't be human if she didn't appreciate the delay. At least the wedding plans wouldn't drain the Kennedys' bank account. Bree planned to wear Alan's grandma's dress, and there wasn't time to buy extras. Thank God.

Mrs. Kennedy looked between Holly and Luke. "And what are *your* plans for tonight?"

She ignored the too-interested tone. "We're having dinner. Catching up on old times."

Mrs. Kennedy smiled. "That's nice. Your fitting's at ten, but come by the house around eight for breakfast."

"Thanks, I will." She kissed her cheek, guilt pressing on

her. Here stood another person who would be devastated to learn Alan had sought out another woman. Holly felt like a destructive force about to demolish the wedding festivities. Hurricane Holly, home for the holidays.

Holly and Luke found seats after a three minute wait. She could feel the speculative gazes as people tried to figure out her identity and her relationship with Luke. A surprisingly varied menu gave her much to consider, as did the man across from her.

After ordering, they caught up on what the other had been doing, her working as assistant marketing director for a leading advertising firm he hadn't heard of and his job as co-owner of the Ivey Orchard.

"Do you and Micah get along okay?" she asked. "Don't you need an official President? What happens when you disagree?"

He shrugged. "We work it out, and if we can't, the idea gets shelved. Neither of us bullies the other into doing something, and I don't pull rank as the older brother. We'd never have survived that."

"I guess." Holly bit into her breaded pork tenderloin sandwich and almost melted. Nowhere in Chicago made one this good. The steak fries on Luke's plate tempted her and she snitched one. Or two. Next time she'd bypass the salad and get these thick salted slabs of heaven.

"So." Luke paused. "Are you seeing anyone?"

She smiled. "Nope. You?"

He trailed a fry through catsup and then smiled back. "Nope."

She shot him an amused glare for making her wait. "Why not?"

"My last girlfriend, about a year ago, liked to see other guys without telling me. It kind of put me off dating. I don't mind keeping an open relationship at the beginning, as long as both parties are honest. But we were past the beginning stage and she wasn't honest."

Holly scowled, thinking of Alan the Cheater and the heartbreak to come when Bree found out. And that she'd have to find out from Holly. "I just don't understand cheating. Either you're in a relationship or you're not."

"I was, she wasn't." He shrugged. "Better to find out early, before we swapped keys."

Holly choked and grabbed her water glass. Must have been a crisp edge of the pork breading. She swallowed half the glassful before catching her breath.

"You okay?"

"Sure." She coughed a little. "Fine. So. You weren't living together?"

He shook his head, munching into his burger.

"But you've lived with someone before?"

"Don't worry, Mom, I'm careful."

She glared at him. "I wasn't asking about your sex life."

"I wasn't telling you about it." He leaned closer, as he'd dropped his voice. "I meant careful about who I give keys to. Careful to get them back. I'm not about to tell you about my sex life."

But when he leaned back, he studied her.

"Why are you looking at me like that?" She picked up her glass, appearing innocent and unconcerned. Or, at least, trying to.

"I'm wondering why you'd want to know about my sex life. And the only reason you'd need to know--the only reason I'd tell you--is if you were next."

She spewed water across the table. She dabbed at her shirt then leaned across the table to mop up his. "Look at this mess. Why'd you say that?"

"Testing the waters. I didn't realize you'd spit those waters all over the place."

"For Pete's sakes, Luke. How did you expect me to react?"

The waitress appeared at their table. "You need some more napkins?"

"No, we're fine." Holly's skin heated with embarrassment.

"Drinking problem," he whispered to the waitress and winked as Holly sputtered indignantly. "She's from Chicago."

He spread his hands in a "what are you going to do" shrug. "Could you bring the check please?"

Holly threw her napkin at him as soon as the waitress turned away. "Thanks a lot."

He laughed. "She knows I'm kidding. She noticed you coughing a minute ago and probably thinks you were choking on the food. She checked on us to avoid a lawsuit."

"It's you I should sue. For reckless endangerment."

He cocked his head. "I'm not driving."

"Your tongue is a weapon."

His lips quirked, then the smile grew as her face burned.

Holly glared. "Don't say it."

"Say what?" His virtuous act didn't fool her. "Do you have anywhere to go now?"

She considered driving to Springfield so she could talk to Bree, but showing up uninvited would be beyond awkward. Why hadn't Bree called now that she was away from the grandma's farm? Holly would be a wreck by the time they connected. "Nope. With Bree gone, I guess I have the evening free."

Luke flipped out his cell phone and eyed the screen. "The Home Town Bazaar is still open for about half an hour. Local groups and businesses offer a variety of items. I thought I'd stop by and waste some money. Want to come with me?"

Holly used the rest room while Luke paid. She fluffed her

hair and fixed the makeup the water had ruined. Reapplying lipstick, she gave herself a strong mental talking to, separating Luke from images of him in bed, and reminding herself not to fall into his mesmerizing, teasing eyes.

They walked along toward the town hall under street lights bedecked with angels, Santas, and reindeer. People milled along, often coming from the hall with bags filled. Storefronts beckoned shoppers. Holly turned her coat collar up against the breeze.

"You need a scarf," Luke said.

"Left it at work."

He put his arm around her shoulders and pulled her closer. "Okay?"

Looking up at him made all her mental reminders fly from her head. He no longer had thick glasses or awkward manners. Not only was he gorgeous, his warmth, friendliness, and the memories of their past lured her in. She nodded. "How did you know all those kids' names back at the cabin?"

"Some families I know, of course. But Micah can ask the parents the names of kids he doesn't recognize. He finger-spelled the ones I signaled I didn't know. Sign language. The alphabet is all either of us know, but it works."

"I didn't notice you guys signing or you giving him any signals."

"Good. You're not supposed to."

"How did you learn it? Why did you learn it?"

"One of Micah's girlfriends taught ASL. He learned sign language to please her, then he realized we could use it for the Santa gig and taught me."

"That's clever. The kids were impressed."

"That's the idea. He's dated a lot of teachers so he knows kids in their classes." Luke grinned. "We both go to schools to talk about farming or trees in particular. We also have field trips out to the orchard, hayrides in the fall, stuff like that."

"Lots of opportunities to interact with the kids."

"Right. Public service and good business."

He guided her into the town hall, which had become a maze of booths and tables. Different associations, clubs and home businesses sold merchandise for gifts and decoration. The Future Farmers of America sat next to the 4-H table. When Luke began a discussion with one of the boys, Holly wandered on a few tables to inspect some homemade soy products. Bree's mother burned candles throughout the year, and Holly's sister, Daisy, would get a kick out of the soaps.

"We have scents for Christmas." The woman behind the table appeared to be Holly's age or a little younger, but Holly didn't recognize her from the past. A pretty blonde, she had cheeks like peaches and cornflower eyes. In a word, she was adorable. She unscrewed a Mason jar and held it out to Holly. "They're made from soybean oil."

Holly sniffed then smiled. "Sugar cookies? What a great idea for the non-cooks of the world." Her apartment could smell like she'd just baked even when she didn't have time.

"We have pumpkin pie scent, apples, cinnamon, and bayberry, of course. Plus others." The woman pointed to jars to Holly's right. "The flower scents are over there, and we have pine-scented, which is popular for anyone who can't have a real tree."

"Hey, now." Luke appeared at Holly's side. "Let's not be spreading that idea around."

The woman smiled. "Sorry, Luke. I meant those poor unfortunates who can't have a tree because they have cats or a baby or don't want the mess."

"Let's leave it at cats and babies, okay, Vicki?"

"Sure thing."

Holly watched Vicki with Luke, speculating on their relationship. Did the other woman lean over the table a little farther now? Smile more winningly? Were she and Luke past lovers? Or did the woman have her sights on the future?

"Vicki Harkins, this is Holly McDonald, an old friend of mine."

An old friend? Despite it being true, the phrase annoyed Holly, so she smiled all the brighter. "Nice to meet you."

"Her older sister was in our class. You remember Joanne."

"Oh, sure." Joanne had been a 4-H winner every year in

their age group, her sewing and baking blue-ribbon quality. A paragon. Seemed that ran in the Harkins family.

"This is my favorite." Vicki unscrewed another jar. "Vanilla icing."

"I need this," Holly declared after inhaling. "One to give away, but one for me. Maybe two for me."

"That's the Christmas spirit," Luke teased.

"I'm supporting the community."

"Yeah," Vicki said, likely detecting a sale, "leave her alone."

Holly wound up with eight jars of candles, mostly for gifts. Her mom would get a kick out of a present from Stilton, too, so she added soaps in luscious honeysuckle and lily of the valley scents.

Two tables down, a lone girl of about ten years sat twirling red yarn through her fingers. Lengths of red, green and white yarn, which appeared to be scarves, lay across the surface. The expression on her face suggested sales had been awful. Or her dog had died.

Holly stopped in front of the girl, who she could see wore a Girl Scout sash sporting only a few badges. Holly could sympathize. This could have been her back in the day. "Hi. What are you selling?"

The girl straightened. "Good evening. I hope you're having fun at the bazaar. My name is Stacy, and I'm from Troop 348."

"Hello, Stacy."

A card taped to the table edge on Stacy's side most likely held the welcome spiel each girl had to recite.

Luke remained silent, eyeing the goods. Holly needed a scarf, but these weren't the quality he had in mind. She deserved cashmere or silk. He wanted to get her something she'd be proud to wear once back in Chicago. Something to remind her of Stilton. Of him.

"We just learned to finger crochet, and the sales of these scarves will help fund our trip to Space Camp." Stacy slumped. "Well, most of the troop learned how. Mine aren't that good. But everyone else's are beautiful."

Holly picked up a red stocking hat and twirled it on a finger. "Who did the caps?"

"Our leader, Mrs. Stoltzski, knitted some and crocheted some to show us different crafts. Then she let us sell those with our stuff. This green scarf is my best friend's. Lori does the badge stuff the best of all of us, as long as we're indoors. She has allergies."

Holly's fingers skated across the green scarf. "This is soft yarn and well made. Which is yours? Since you're doing time behind the table, I'd like to see your work."

"No, you wouldn't. Trust me. Lori's are better."

Luke cocked his head. "Now I'm curious, too. Let's see them."

With great reluctance, Stacy pulled a yellow canvas tote bag from under the table. "You asked for it."

Out spilled knots of yarn with holes bigger than the other crocheted pieces. Luke surmised they weren't original to the pattern. One solid red scarf wrapped around several multi-colored ones. They were, in a word, horrific.

"I like these." Holly unearthed the pile of red, white and green.

Typical Holly. Rooting for the underdog.

"Mrs. Stoltzski said those won't sell. She didn't want me to get those colors. It's called variegated yarn. I didn't alternate them myself." Stacy separated the strands from one scarf. "See, they're dyed, not knotted together."

Holly frowned. "Why won't they sell?"

"Because they're not practical. They're not red or white or green but all of them. And you can't wear it any time but Christmas."

"Hmm."

Luke stiffened, ready for a classic Holly McDonald lambasting of the leader. Holly had never had patience for "rules" of fashion--or rules of much else, as he recalled. She hadn't been shy about voicing that impatience either.

"I see what she means." Holly set down the red hat.

Luke relaxed.

"But I disagree."

Oh, crap.

"See this pin?" Holly pointed to her lapel where an enamel snowman smiled. When the girl nodded, Holly pointed to her earrings. "And these? I certainly can't wear Rudolph any other time of the year. But I enjoy decorating myself for the holidays, as much as decorating a tree or my apartment. It's festive."

"I guess."

Stacy's leader had certainly brainwashed the girl. She wouldn't be easily won over. He couldn't wait to watch Holly try.

"This scarf, having all the holiday colors, will brighten up my black coat. When I'm done with it, I can put it away with my holiday jewelry and sweatshirts." Holly snapped her fingers. "And I can wear it to Italian Fest, since these are the colors on the Italian flag."

She turned to Luke. "What are the flag colors for Mexico? Aren't they red, white and green also? Because I could wear this for Cinco de Mayo." She looked back to the girl. "I live in Chicago where it's chilly to downright cold three quarters of the year, so I often need extra layers."

"You do?" The girl soaked in Holly's reassurance with worshipful eyes.

Obviously Holly excelled at winning over young girls. And grown men. Luke couldn't help but marvel at the change in his now-wiser friend. The old Holly would have gone off on the leader for being insensitive, undermining the woman's authority and placing the girl in the middle. He admired Holly's restraint.

"I need one for myself right now," Holly said, "because I left my scarf at work in Chicago. I won't be able to get it until after Christmas, and my neck and ears will be frozen off by then."

"Okay."

"Another present for you?" Luke smiled at Holly.

"I deserve something special. It's not impractical," she assured the girl. "You should put that on a tent card. 'Something extra for that special holiday feel...because you deserve it.' What do you think?"

"I..."

"Right. Not good enough." Holly shook her head. "Let's see. 'Warm up your holidays...because you deserve it.' Does that work?"

"Sure, I guess."

"Do you have a marker?"

"I don't think so." Stacy frowned and searched the cash box. "No."

"Wait. Let me look." Holly rifled through her briefcase-sized purse. "I usually have... Got it. Oh, my gosh, it's red. That's a sign, for sure. A sign about the sign."

She laughed and the girl joined in. Luke shook his head.

The females folded and refolded paper until a sturdy tent emerged. Holly wrote out the words with beautiful, calligraphy-quality handwriting.

"Shouldn't we add the price?" Stacy asked. "Mrs. Stoltzski's hats cost more than scarves because there are so few of them."

"Hmm." A wealth of disapproval for the leader layered the sound. "No, let's see if you can lure buyers with just the sign, then zing them with the price once they're here. Now, I'm going to need a few of these variegated ones that you made."

"Really?" The girl's wide eyes expressed awe.

"Definitely. Me, my mom, my sister, my best friend." Holly turned to Luke. "What about Micah's girlfriend? If she's getting sick from her sister, she wouldn't have come tonight and probably won't have one of these scarves. Anyone else you can think of that needs some color and cheer?"

"Bree's mom?"

Holly grinned. "Good idea."

"And I'll take the red hat." Luke ignored Holly's scowl as he purchased the leader's craft. "I have a few friends, too."

"That's all my scarves." Stacy's words came out on one long breath, filled with wonder. Her face shone with delight.

"You better get busy." Holly nodded to the yarn the girl had set aside.

"I thought this red one might work for Valentine's Day."

"Excellent idea. What do I owe you?"

Paid up and loaded down with the poorest made scarves ever crafted, Holly swung her new scarf around her shoulders. Luke lifted her hair, the weight like heavy silk, so she could tuck the scarf into her collar.

"Perfect," she said.

He agreed, although about Holly more than the knot of yarn. And what a mess that feeling might lead to.

He took the bag of candles from her. "You know you don't have time to mail these things, right?"

She shrugged. "They'll make nice pick-me-ups in the cold of January."

Luke smiled. She'd bought these "gifts" to support the community and encourage a young girl. With such a generous spirit, no wonder he felt like a catfish being reeled to the bank. She'd hooked him.

Would having a fling with Holly ruin their memories? There wasn't any point to starting something when she'd be going back to Chicago in a few days. He didn't have the time or inclination to manage a long distance relationship.

And this was *Holly*. He couldn't think of her as just some woman to have a fling with. How deep did his attraction to her go? Was he prepared to think about forever, and wooing her into returning to Stilton to live?

"Ready?" she asked.

"I believe I am."

CHAPTER FOUR

Holly speculated on Luke's silence as they strolled back to the car. What had she done to put that frown between his brows? Once they reached the Corolla, she set her purchases in the back seat, closed the door and turned, only to discover her body brushing his.

"Would you like to go back to my house?" he asked. "Maybe have some wine? Continue that catching up you told Anne we'd be doing?"

"Sure." She kept her voice steady. Bree's mom had read more into the phrase than Holly had meant. At the time. Although now, after spending the evening with Luke, she wanted to see if they had chemistry. Not like when they played with his junior scientist set, and it blew them up. Just the kind of chemistry that set adults on fire.

And where would that lead? They lived in different worlds, and she couldn't see Luke in hers. Chicago had little, if any, need for a tree farmer.

"Wait a minute." Luke pulled something from his pocket.

He pulled the Girl Scout leader's red cap over her head. "Can't have the maid of honor catching a cold."

Holly scowled and whipped it off. "That woman made this. Then told an impressionable young girl hers weren't good enough."

He yanked the cap back on her, cupping her ears to keep it in place. "Forget her. This is from me. Wearing it means you acknowledge our friendship and my right to worry about your health because we're important to each other. Always were, still are."

"You're manipulating my feelings."

"You're right." He grinned. "Is it working?"

"No." But she left the cap on.

She followed his directions, all the while trying to hide her frown. He'd left their old neighborhood for one with multi-use housing. A single family dwelling sat across from a townhouse. Sitting in his driveway, she studied his duplex. "I imagined you living near Madison Avenue where we grew up."

That he'd moved away, moved on, disconcerted her. She'd envisioned Stilton remaining the same, like Brigadoon, waiting for her return.

"Micah and I moved out before Dad died, then neither of us wanted to move back in with all those memories. We sold the old place." He, too, studied the duplex. "Sometimes I wish we hadn't. But this makes sense for us now. Micah has the half on the right, and we did some renovations. Come see."

She trailed behind him, noting the decorations the guys had strung. Lights lined the roofline and wound around the railing on the shared porch. Both doors held wreaths. "These are nice."

Luke unlocked the door. "They're from our store, of course. Free advertising. I usually go in through the garage. Let me give the front room a quick once-over."

She entered, somehow knowing his house would be neat enough for company, if not earning merit on a white glove test. The great room held typical bachelor furniture--big TV, long leather couch with a pull for a reclining section, two other recliner chairs, a glass coffee table full of remotes, speakers and music docks. The overflowing floor to ceiling bookcase surprised her but shouldn't have. Drawn, she studied his titles while he messed--or unmessed--around in the kitchen. Mysteries dominated, along with men's adventure and many NYT bestsellers. On an over-her-head shelf he could probably reach with ease sat textbooks on all the sciences. Computer guides sidled up to home repair DIY books.

"I'm envious." She turned as he entered with two wine glasses. He'd shed his coat and looked warm and inviting for an evening at home. She could picture him cuddled on the couch. With her. Maybe watching a movie as they sipped what she discovered was a crisp apple-flavored wine. "I like this."

"Local product. Not apples from our orchard, but Gary's a nice enough guy, so we don't hold it against him."

She smiled and set her glass on the coffee table. Shedding her coat made her self-conscious, and she chastised herself for being silly. He'd seen her earlier-- Heavens, had it just been a few hours before that she'd pulled off the highway?

She set her shoulders, determined to either move their relationship on to a new level or rescue their old friendship. "Give me the tour? You can explain what you changed."

"This is the living room. That's the kitchen." He pointed with a smile, since he didn't have to move for the presentation. "Behind the stairs is the mud room which leads to the garage. We moved the washer and dryer there since we come home pretty dirty sometimes."

"Is Micah's half like this?" Holly wandered to a door below the stairs. "Powder room?"

"Yes, to both. His downstairs half is flipped so our shared wall is his kitchen, too. Saved on plumbing to have all the pipes together."

"Okay." She could envision it. "What about upstairs?"

"Over the powder room here is a full bathroom, which is in the guest bedroom." He started for the stairs then gestured her ahead of him.

Did he watch her walk up? Of course he did. He was male, after all. The thought gave her a little thrill and made her extremely self-conscious.

He's always seen you as a best buddy, though. Her internal devil's advocate chimed in to ruin her fun. Luke probably wasn't looking at her rear, at all. Darn it.

At the top, she stepped onto a tiny landing. Two doors led off on opposite sides. A window lit the shared space and a table with a mirror above gave it a cozy feel. She wondered if the suggestion for the table and mirror came from a girlfriend. Luke didn't strike her as the type to watch decorating shows after a hard day's work.

He gestured to the right. She opened the door to a nice-sized room with a queen bed covered in a navy spread. A cherry wood antique dresser and mirror sat across from it, while a small table beside the bed served as a nightstand. Close enough in style and color to the headboard, she'd have thought the three pieces were a matching set. "Nice job on the furniture."

"Thanks. We were lucky. The woman Micah was dating when we finished renovations fancied going to estate sales and antiquing." He grinned. "She also liked to refinish furniture."

"That Micah sure has a list of accomplished lady friends."

"He has a list, all right."

Holly tilted her head in question. Were Luke and Micah still playing the field? Being bachelor brothers and breaking hearts all over town? "Is Micah looking to settle down or is he just looking for fun?"

"He'll drop like a stone in a creek when he meets the right girl. He's born to be a husband and father, run the Orchard until he hands it off to his kids, and probably run for mayor."

She took a fortifying breath. "And you? Are you destined to be a dad and a town father?"

"I'm not a politician. Micah's got the charm."

"You're plenty charming."

He grinned. "Oh, you think so?"

"Yes, and I think you only answered half the question."

Gazing into her eyes, he put one hand on her waist, paused, and cupped the other hand at her hip. Close enough to sense her heart racing, she thought. "I'm just as old-fashioned. I've got no aspirations to be more than what I am, except to make some woman happy someday, and have a bunch of kids if we're lucky enough." He ran a finger down her cheek. "I'd love to raise a spirited tomboy or a frilly girly-girl. Or both."

"Both?" The word came out on a breath. She could picture him with a tomboy, of course, since he'd spent years with her. But the image of gentle Luke with a delicate, curly-headed daughter nearly brought tears to her eyes. He'd be a great dad.

"And some boys," he added. "I'll need some help looking after those girls. Chasing off potential boyfriends."

"I can see that. You with a brood. Kissing their boo boos. Helping with homework after a long day at the orchard. Teaching them to drive. Lecturing them about safe sex."

He laughed and stepped back. "Whoa. My kids are growing up way too fast."

"So, why aren't you married? You own a business, have a nice home, aren't terrifying to look at. What's the hold up?"

"I came close a couple of times, but things never quite gelled. I've looked." He smirked. "Maybe not as diligently as Micah. I'll know when I've found the right partner, and I'll fall hard and fast."

"So you're picky?"

"You bet I am. We're talking about forever here, Holly. I only plan to marry once."

Good news: Luke wanted a family. Bad news: he wanted a family living in Stilton. Holly couldn't see where she fit into the picture.

But, oh, how she wanted to. Envisioning Luke as a dad, maybe an extension of his patience and humor posing as Santa, made her yearn to be part of it. Unfortunately, he wouldn't move, and she couldn't live in this small town. She wouldn't be able to find work here. The commute to Chicago would be four hours each day. She'd never see those kids he was so excited about having.

Heck, she'd never be in Stilton long enough to conceive them.

So friends it would be. She gave him a bright no-big-deal smile. "Is that your room across the hall?"

"Yeah." After a second look that challenged the no-big-deal to stay steady, he shrugged and turned.

Holly took ten seconds to mourn what might have been then followed.

The other bedroom encompassed more than half the upstairs. A king size bed, unmade and inviting, dominated the space. His oak furnishings were more contemporary and square, which suited him. He was a straight-forward guy, without dusty nooks or irritating crannies. Sturdy. Another bookcase, also crammed, sat across the room, with a comfortable reading chair, floor lamp and small table beside it.

"Another TV?" she asked, after spotting it behind the slightly ajar door of an entertainment cabinet she'd mistaken for an armoire.

He grinned. "A guy gets sick."

She smirked. "A guy gets lazy."

"Guilty. But it's nice to watch a movie or sports late into the night without having to get up to go to bed afterward. Or early in the rare morning when I don't have to work and I'm feeling--yes--lazy."

"I guess it's better than sleeping on the sofa."

"I can sleep anywhere."

"I remember that," she said. "You were the first one asleep when we went camping. I'm envious. Despite all our travels during my childhood, it always takes me a week or so to settle in."

"Vacations must be hell for you."

"I don't do many. Out to see my parents or the sibs, but their homes are familiar, so I can fall sleep by the second or third night. Then I'm usually headed home." She walked over to the inner door, hoping to change the subject. Her sleeping quirks annoyed her. She should be able to overcome them. "Is this a bathroom or closet?"

Opening the door all the way answered her question. A huge bathroom, with separate shower and tub. "Are those jets? In the shower *and* the tub?"

"My muscles get sore." Luke didn't add that, with a partner, they could provide fun in places that didn't ache from tiredness. Holly had put up the "just friends" sign, and he respected it. Didn't especially like it, but he respected it.

For a minute, in the hall, with her in his arms, and them talking about kids in the far-off future, he'd thought she'd been receptive to more than friendship. Not that he meant marriage and kids and the whole shebang right now. Not yet. But he thought he'd read interest on her face, warmth in her voice, acceptance in her embrace. Longing in her eyes.

Maybe he couldn't read his old pal as well as he used to. Maybe only he considered the possibility of them as a couple.

Which would be crazy, with her living so far away. So that was that.

"The kitchen is right below," he said, "so, again, the plumbing was handy. Micah's guest room shares my bedroom wall. It's soundproof, but we didn't want to live in each other's pockets. Sometimes even this much togetherness is too much."

"I can imagine."

"However, we do share a patio with sliders opening from our kitchens. That's handy for whoever gets home first with meat."

She laughed, as he'd meant her to. There. Balance restored. "Let's go get that wine."

They reversed their trip, and Luke regretted he'd been admiring her backside. That crossed the line for friends. Even though his friend had a killer butt that he'd like to-- *No. Stop. Friends.*

With the "just old pals" reminder in place, he settled into the recliner with relief. The leather welcomed him as it did every night. Holly curled up on the sofa, falling into her old pattern of tucking her feet up to the side. Give her a book and a lemonade, fashion a set of braids or a ponytail, and he'd be hard pressed to remember any time had passed.

"You were real nice to that Girl Scout," he said.

She sipped her wine. "What did you expect?"

"Honestly? I thought you'd berate her leader for insensitivity."

"I did. I just kept it in my head instead of letting it burst out of my mouth."

He tilted his glass toward hers. "To new habits."

"Very funny." But she clinked glasses with him anyway. "Speaking of the bazaar, have you been involved with...the FFA?"

He thought she'd started to ask about Vicki and couldn't help but be disappointed that she wasn't curious. "My cousin, Bob's son, is in FFA."

"I didn't realize anyone wanted to be a farmer anymore."

Luke stiffened. "I'm a farmer."

"Right. Sorry. I just meant it's different for you and Micah. You inherited the orchard and Christmas trees, so it's the family business." She shrugged. "It's harder for corn, wheat or soy farmers, isn't it? Limited government subsidies. Farms dying out. Drought. Heat. Hail."

He scowled at her depressing picture of his life. "Don't forget it freezing late in the Spring."

"Right."

She made the life sound less than appealing. What was so great about Chicago? Cheering for the Cubs? He snorted. "We have fresh air."

"Sorry. I shouldn't have said anything. I guess if you grow up here, it's different. You don't know anything else." Holly groaned and squeezed her eyes shut, missing his glare. "I didn't mean that the way it sounded either."

He took a large swallow, finishing off his wine. "You didn't mean it to sound how? As though only fools who don't know what opportunities the Big City offers would stay tied to the land?"

"No. Luke, that's not what I meant."

"I went to college, Holly. So did Micah."

"I know. I'm sorry. I mean, I didn't know for sure about the college part, but I'm not surprised you went."

"We chose this life."

"You were always smart."

"Dad told us to sell if it wasn't what we wanted."

She knelt beside his chair and put a soft warm hand on the fist he hadn't been aware of making. "I'm sorry, Luke. I love the Ivey Orchard and Christmas Tree Farm. I always have. I meant no disrespect to your family's business or you and your brother."

Her cheek settled on his fist, her hands cupping his. Large dark eyes stared up at him, repentant. "Or the town or your friends."

After a moment, he took a breath and let his go of his frustration. She had a different set of values. Her underscoring that shouldn't bother him.

Shouldn't.

But it did.

"It's getting late, and I need some sleep to fortify me for

tomorrow." Holly stood up and stretched. "I better go see if the hotel saved me a room."

"You didn't guarantee late check-in?"

She shook her head. "I wasn't sure when I'd get here. If it was early enough, I thought I'd stay with Bree. We have some things to talk about that could have taken all night."

"You're just like Anne. If you'd made plans, Bree wouldn't have gone to Springfield."

"She didn't know I wanted to have a serious discussion."

Luke smirked. "I think she's heard about the birds and the bees."

"I'd rather she'd heard about latex and sponges."

He laughed. "She's not pregnant, is she? Is that behind the rushed wedding? Alan didn't mention that."

"God, I hope not." Holly shook her head, forestalling his question. "It's not the right time to think about building their family. And since I'm talking without making sense to you, I better go."

"Or...you could stay here."

Holly jerked her head toward him, stunned. She lingered at the "let's see if we're attracted to each other" stage, not the sleepover stage.

The word "sleepover" gave her pause. She sank onto the chair opposite him. Was it handsome, bewitching Luke propositioning her or her old pal Luke suggesting she'd had a long day? Was she reading something more into his offer because she was attracted to him?

She would refuse either offer, she realized, not yet ready to have sex with him, despite their knowing each other since childhood. She also needed some thinking time before she saw Bree.

She barely stopped herself from saying as a joke, "I haven't had that much wine." Old Pal Luke would be appeased. Propositioning Luke would be insulted. She sighed. When had things become so complicated?

Because it would be more than "just" sex with Luke, no matter her earlier ideas about a fling. Old Pal Luke meant too much to her and Grownup Luke had already turned her head and carved a separate place in her heart.

"Those wheels are turning." Luke wore a grin. "I can hear the grind of the gears from here."

Her face heated. Was it more embarrassing that Old Pal Luke guessed she'd considered having sex with him or that Grownup Luke knew? A close tie, she decided.

"Let me make this easier on you," he said.

I wish you would.

He rose and knelt beside her chair, eyes intent on hers. Her mouth went dry as he reached for her hand. Could he feel her pulse racing?

"I have..." He raised her hand to his lips. His Ivey blue

eyes darkened as he kissed her fingers. "A guest room."

It took her a minute to separate his words from his actions. Relief warred with disappointment.

He chuckled. "You should see your face."

"You're hilarious."

"Holly, when I make a move on you, you'll know it."

She held his gaze. A moment passed as tension thickened in the air between them. "Are you planning to make a move?"

He nodded. "I'm thinking about it. Would that be...weird for you?"

She considered. "I'll think about it."

"You do that." He surged up over her, a hand on each arm of the chair, making her retreat into the back cushion. He crowded her space without touching her anywhere. "Here's something else to think about."

His mouth covered hers, their only touching point. Fire spread from her lips to her cheeks, to ears, to hair roots. Her chest heated, her fingertips tingled. He pulled back, breathing hard, just before her socks ignited.

"Think fast," he said.

She grinned. "I don't know. It's a pretty big decision."

Pushing himself all the way up to his feet, he blew out a breath. "No rush. We have three whole days."

The wedding was in two days, on Sunday afternoon. *Would have been.* Holly sighed. "I'm going to be busy tomorrow."

"Lots of activities planned for the wedding," Luke agreed, not knowing there probably wouldn't be a wedding. "Micah is taking over for me in the afternoon so I can help Alan get ready for the dinner at Romero's."

"Bree's expecting me for breakfast, so I better head out."

"No, she's not," Luke said. "Bree's in Springfield. She'll eat before she leaves there. Why don't you call Anne and tell her you'll come later in the morning?"

"I don't know." But Holly checked her watch. Eleven o'clock. "She might be in bed."

"Text her. If she's in bed already, she'll read it tomorrow." He leaned closer. "I make a mean pancake. Real fluffy. Lots of butter and syrup."

Giving in, she affected a French accent. "I am not conveenced, Chef Luc. Do you have zee references for zeese cakes o' pan?"

He shrugged, spreading his hands in a Gallic gesture. She delighted they could still play off each other like a comedy duo.

"You have my ward," he said in his own faux-French. "But if you like, you may call a few of my past *bonnes amies*. Eh, how do you say...my girlfriends?"

Even as she blushed, she laughed at having set herself up by asking for references. She could too easily picture him making "morning after" breakfast for some woman. Women.

"Here we are again, talking about your sex life."

"Not yet we aren't." He waggled his eyebrows. "But I have hope." He held his palm out. "In the meantime, let me grab your suitcase from your car."

She retrieved her keys from her purse before she argued herself out of staying. Driving anywhere right then held no appeal. The big bed upstairs did. Climbing into her pajamas did. Seeing Luke in the morning certainly did.

She texted Anne Kennedy who called back right away, sounding too knowing, too understanding and entirely too encouraging. Holly shook her head as Luke came back inside.

"What?" he asked. "Does that 'no' mean don't bring your bag in?"

"Bree's mom is matchmaking. I think the romance of the wedding planning has gone to her head."

Luke set down her suitcase and came to stand before her, not quite invading her space but close. "Should I ask who she's matching up?"

"Take one guess."

"Us?"

Holly nodded.

"Is that out of the question? Because I'd like to know if you've already made up your mind against us."

He stood, tense. Fighting the urge to touch her?

"Against us?" Her voice came out rusty. "I'm leaving on

Christmas night, Luke. Maybe earlier." *Once I break my friend's heart and ruin the wedding.* "We don't have time to become a couple. An 'us.'"

"So you haven't decided anything? It's just the problem of time keeping you from exploring the possibilities?"

"Time and distance. Two factors, Einstein, which work against us, no matter what we want."

He grinned. "Time is relative."

She rolled her eyes, wishing she hadn't invoked the Father of Relativity to the science geek. Luke would just use Albert's wisdom against her.

"Distance," he continued, "is perspective."

"Whose theory is that?"

"Mine. And probably someone famous." He framed her face in his palms, making her heart race. "Let's see what happens, Holly, okay? Then we'll worry about overcoming obstacles."

She nodded and he kissed her lightly, as though sealing the deal.

"I'll take your bag up," he said.

To which room?

She grinned, knowing Luke. No matter the time or distance that had separated them, she understood his basic character. And she knew where she'd be laying her head.

CHAPTER FIVE

December 22nd

The next morning, Holly stumbled into the kitchen, still in her robe and pajamas, but with freshly scrubbed face and teeth and brushed hair. Makeup had seemed a bit too obvious. She didn't want to show him her morning-hag face, but neither did she want to seem to be trying to impress him.

"Morning." Luke didn't turn from the stove where bacon popped. "Did you get any sleep?"

"Yes, surprisingly enough. Your guest room is comfy." She'd lain awake for a while either worrying about how to tell Bree about Alan or wondering what to do about her unexpected attraction to Luke. Managing to get three hours of sleep in a strange bed would have been a bonus under normal circumstances. Given these circumstances, three hours felt like winning the lottery.

"I was just going to call you down," Luke said.

"No need. I was drawn down here by a powerful lure."

"Bacon sizzling?"

She shook her head.

A slow, sexy smile grew on his face. "Me?"

She shook her head.

He frowned playfully. "What could be more alluring than me if it's not bacon?"

"Coffee."

"Help yourself. Cups are up there." He pointed toward a cabinet with the tongs he used to turn bacon. "I'm about to make the pancakes."

Batter sat in a white ceramic mixing bowl beside the stove. The cheery yellow kitchen featured new appliances and plenty of counter space. Light oak cupboards would hold supplies enough for a large family, though many of Luke's shelves stood empty.

He'd showered, shaved and wore jeans and a red cable knit sweater. Had he dressed to impress her? The idea elicited a tingle of pleasure.

Holly glanced at the wall clock which depicted a different songbird at each hour. Seven-thirty. Too early to show up at the Kennedys for her fitting, but time enough to check in at the hotel.

"I have to leave for work soon," he said, obviously noting her glance at the clock. "We open in an hour, and I've got the day shift. Micah's working this afternoon to free me up for the dinner and the rehearsal."

"You might be free tonight anyway."

Holly couldn't believe she'd spoken aloud. Not wanting to pursue that conversation, she asked in a rush, "Are there many customers buying trees so close to Christmas?"

Luke studied her for a minute while she held her breath.

"Yes," he said, letting her change the subject, much to her relief. "Enough people shop at the last minute to keep us hopping. They buy poinsettias they don't want to get too early for fear of killing them. Evergreen trim for their gifts or a wreath for a hostess gift. Some customers don't put up a tree until the twenty-fourth, so we're always busy."

She sipped her coffee, the hot jab welcome to her sleepy body. "Do they want the forlorn look of Charlie Brown's Christmas tree? Because I can't imagine there's much choice left."

He flipped the hotcakes. "Some leave it to chance, but others purchase their tree early and leave it with us. Then it doesn't dry out at their homes."

"That's a good idea." Holly wrapped her hands around the warm mug. She grinned at the image of a St. Bernard on the cup, noting the barrel around his neck labeled "Caffeine." Most mornings, she'd welcome Cujo into her bedroom if he brought her hot coffee.

As they ate, they talked more about the orchard, her

adventures entering a different school each time her family moved, and a little bit about Luke's mom passing from breast cancer when he was nineteen.

"She never saw Micah graduate from high school." Luke topped off their cups. "It's a shame he spent so few years with her. But he had Dad all to himself while I went to college."

"Where did you go?"

"U of I for Agriculture. Champaign felt like a world away from here for me. I only made it home for the major holidays." He stared into his mug. "If I'd known I'd only have a couple more years with Dad, I'd have come more often."

"I was sorry to hear about his passing."

"I got your card and the flowers, Holly. It was thoughtful of you to send them after all those years."

"He was a great man. So patient with us both, and he and your mom accepted me into your lives like a daughter." She thought of how his parents and Bree's mom had filled in for her less-attentive parents. "I've been very lucky in my life. I hoped when you read my name, some memories would return to comfort you."

"They did. I even said to Micah, 'wouldn't Dad get a kick out of knowing Holly remembered him?' And Dad would have."

"He should have expected it of me. So should you."

"Time passes." Luke held her gaze.

"Some things don't change."

He took her hand. "Something's about to."

"Maybe."

"I mean our friends getting married."

She stiffened and sat up straight, but he didn't release her.

"Holly, what did you mean by that remark earlier? That I might have tonight free? Tonight is the dinner Alan's parents are hosting."

The pancakes sat like lead in her stomach. The syrup tasted too sweet in her mouth and the milk too warm. In short, she felt like throwing up.

She had to make a decision. Wanting Bree to hear the news first was admirable. Needing to share her burden was selfish. She swallowed hard and took a breath. She could trust Luke not to gossip so telling him wouldn't affect Bree, and maybe he could help her with the wording. Right now she could only blurt, "Alan cheated on Bree."

Luke dropped her hand as though he held poison oak. "What?"

"Alan cheated on Bree."

"How do you know? I mean, you must be mistaken."

How did she know? Did he know too? She searched his gaze but he seemed genuinely surprised, not covering for his friend. "I saw him."

His eyes went wide. "You saw him having sex?"

"Of course not. I saw him going into the Palmer House Hotel with a woman."

Luke slumped in his chair and ran a hand over his face. "Holy crap, Holly, you had me worried there for a minute."

"What do you mean, for a minute?"

"Think how many reasons there could be for a man and woman to walk into a hotel--in the middle of downtown, mind you, not out at some no-tell motel on the fringes of nowhere. Just seeing him with another woman doesn't mean he did anything wrong."

She clenched her teeth. It didn't surprise her that Luke would defend his friend, but she'd hoped for support, for outrage on Bree's behalf. Instead she got the good old boy network sticking together, assuming she must be mistaken.

"Was it during the day?" Luke asked. "Doesn't the Palmer House have a restaurant? Maybe it was a business meeting. Alan sees clients outside the office all the time."

She narrowed her eyes and leaned toward him. "I don't really care about Alan's work habits, Luke. It's his personal arrangements I object to."

"Okay, calm down. What did you see?"

Calm down? She was likely to kick him under the table. She'd labored like Hercules over her decision whether to tell Bree. But then they'd announced the quickie wedding and she couldn't dally. "Isn't it enough that I'm telling you I saw him with that woman? That it's me saying it?"

"Of course it matters that it's you accusing him, Holly. I know you'd never say it if you didn't believe it." He blew out a breath. "But, I'm sorry, it's kind of circumstantial. He walked into a public place with a female. That hardly merits putting him on death row."

"With his arm around her."

Luke dipped his head, conceding the point. "Okay, with his arm around her. It's still not conclusive."

She scowled. "You should have been the lawyer instead of him."

"I wouldn't have been able to stand working inside. What else do you have for proof?"

My word. She crossed her arms, too hurt to continue. His questions weren't unreasonable, and she realized her anger stemmed from having no concrete evidence. She hadn't thought she'd need it, and she'd been too stunned at the time to think of taking a picture with her phone. Now she wondered if Bree would need more than her word, too.

"I'm guessing she was our age," Luke said into the silence, "perhaps even attractive. You wouldn't be getting all hot and bothered over some dowager."

"I'm not sure what her face looked like. I was at an angle and too busy confirming it was Alan."

Luke smiled. "Could have been a relative then. His

cousin."

"His kissing cousin?"

Luke's smile faltered.

"His groping-her-breast-on-the-street cousin?"

"Are you sure?"

"His caressing-her-fanny cousin?"

"In public?" Luke sat back again.

"Yes. Luke, I saw him do all those things. Judging by her shape and clothes, I'd say she's our age or just a bit younger. And I moved to see Alan's face, straight on. No doubt it was him." She sighed. "I wouldn't be telling Bree about it if I wasn't sure."

"I know that. I know you believe what you saw, but, Holly, there are always things going on in other people's relationships that--"

"It was Monday."

Luke's jaw dropped. Vindication arced through her despite the misery of the circumstances. He finally understood the gravity of the problem.

"Last Monday?" he said incredulously. "This past Monday?"

She nodded.

"Two days before he proposed to Bree?"

She waited while he swore, while he talked himself into believing it possible, then out of it again. While he cursed Alan and lamented over poor Bree. It took about a minute. Luke knew his mind, knew right from wrong.

"What do you plan to do about it?" he asked.

"I'm telling Bree, of course."

"You think that's the right option?"

Holly blinked. Maybe only Old Pal Luke knew right from wrong. "Yes, I do. Why? What do you think I should do?"

"How about...nothing?"

She jumped to her feet. "Nothing?"

He pushed himself up slowly, using the table for support, as though riddled with arthritis. "Holly--"

"That rat bastard cheater is about to marry my best friend and break her heart, and you expect me to do *nothing?*"

"Wait a minute."

She stepped out of his reach. If he touched her now, she'd elbow him in the nose like she'd learned in her self-defense class. Then stomp on his instep. Disgust and disappointment eroded her respect for him. How could he expect her to let Alan get away scot-free?

A tap sounded on the glass door, loud as gunfire. Luke and Holly both jumped and spun. Micah's eyes widened, his hand frozen in mid-knock.

"It's just Micah," Luke said unnecessarily. He crossed to the sliding door, unsure whether he was glad for the interruption. He couldn't trust Holly not to run straight to Bree and tell her the whole sordid story.

Not that he would blame her. If Alan had cheated, he was a despicable bastard, as Holly had said. Bree was too nice a woman to do that to--not that anyone deserved it, but Bree least of all. Having been in her place with an unfaithful partner, Luke could sympathize. But would it do any good to tell Bree? Wouldn't knowing ruin her happiness, even if Alan never cheated again?

He had a few words to exchange with his buddy, which was pretty much what Holly planned with her friend. The difference was Luke wanted reassurance Alan had this fling out of his system and would be faithful from here out. Holly expected Bree to jilt Alan, practically at the altar.

Micah stepped inside. "Am I interrupting anything?"

"What would you do if I said yes?" Luke asked wryly.

"I'd fill a plate with pancakes and bacon to eat at my place. Good morning, Holly."

"Hi. Help yourself to breakfast." She speared Luke with a look so withering, he blinked in surprise. "I think we're done here."

She turned, outrage vibrating off her.

"Don't do anything rash," Luke called. "Please."

She waved him off, but at least she used all five fingers to do it. He considered that a good sign.

"Did I come at a bad time?" Micah asked.

"Not really. Earlier would have been bad. I think we were done talking."

"How did things go last night?"

"Well, Star Night was a success."

Micah's mouth twisted. "Yeah, 'cause that's what I was asking about."

"Overall, it was good. Holly and I caught up on our time apart. We might have been going forward. I'm not sure." Luke shifted under Micah's gaze then glanced at the clock. He had no time to mend things with Holly, if he even could. "Did we stay busy last night?"

"Not after Santa left. Everyone wanted to get into town to the ceremony."

"Right." Luke looked around the counter, patted his pockets. His keys were in his coat. His car was at the Orchard store lot. "Dammit."

"You taking off?" Micah didn't quite hide a smile.

"Yeah." Luke poured coffee into his travel mug then held out the pot to offer some to his brother. At Micah's nod, he grabbed another cup.

"I guess Holly's not taking you to work." Micah glanced at the ceiling, the room above eerily silent. "You getting a ride in or taking my car?"

"I'll take yours, if you don't need it."

"Sure, I'm working around home today. I'll need a ride in

later, though."

"I'll send Cindy to get you."

Micah groaned. "Not Cindy. She's overly perfumed, overly made up, and overly talkative."

Luke held back a smile, knowing why Micah objected. "She's sixteen."

"She pops her gum."

"You're just nervous because she has a crush on you."

Micah scowled. "As you said, she's sixteen. Send Sean to get me."

He couldn't resist needling his brother. "I'll see who's available."

"Send Sean or get your own ride this morning. You should have driven your car home last night anyway."

"Maybe."

"But then you wouldn't have been with Holly." Micah said nothing for a moment. "I saw her car in your driveway. All night." He paused again, no doubt waiting for Luke to elaborate. When Luke said nothing, he grinned. "Spill it, bro. I know she didn't just show up for breakfast."

"Guest room," Luke answered his brother's unvoiced question. Used to each other, they could read the other's thoughts and moods. Which is how Luke knew his brother understood he didn't want to talk about Holly. Whether Micah would respect that wish remained to be seen.

"Whose idea?" Micah asked.

Luke frowned. Micah didn't usually pry. "Both of ours."

Micah raised his eyebrows.

"For now. We weren't sure where this was going last night." Luke blew out a breath, thinking of her plan to break up Alan and Bree's wedding. He didn't doubt her motivation...exactly. But how much of the integrity of twelve-year-old Holly remained in this woman he hadn't seen for fifteen years? "Today, I doubt there's a 'this' to go anywhere with. She's stubborn and over-opinionated. And she's leaving soon. Which reminds me, can you take her suitcase down to her car for her? I don't think she wants to see me right now."

Micah nodded but didn't say anything. Luke figured he debated the wisdom of asking why Luke had decided not to pursue Holly. Neither of them liked talking about their feelings.

"Sure you can't fix it?" Micah asked.

Luke shrugged, relieved not to have to explain the details. He wouldn't brush off his brother's concern, but he didn't want to expose Holly's plan. He needed to talk to Alan first of anyone.

As far as him and Holly getting past this? He'd been surprised by Holly's vehement insistence on telling Bree. Would he have wanted someone to tell him Sara stepped out on him before he'd caught her doing it? He hadn't liked hearing about it after he'd known, so he doubted he'd have wanted to find out that way. Gossip seemed to benefit the teller of bad news, not the recipient. He couldn't imagine Holly having such an unattractive trait.

But did it count as gossip if it was true? Given Holly's insistence, he had to believe she'd witnessed Alan at least kissing--and groping--another woman. Didn't Holly have Bree's best interest at heart, not wanting her saddled with a cheating husband? Or was she just poking her nose where it didn't belong? The whole situation confused him, which in turn pissed him off. "I'm not sure I want to fix anything with her. I'm not sure of much at all right now."

"Man, I'm sorry. I always liked Holly, and you seemed to be having fun yesterday playing Santa and Mrs. Claus."

"We did. But not everything is fun." Like his upcoming talk with Alan.

"What in the hell were you thinking?" Luke demanded an hour later, standing in his office at the Orchard. He'd called Alan and asked him to come out, since Luke couldn't leave. His employees were as busy as Santa's reindeer on Christmas Eve, rushing every which way to fill orders.

Alan stuck his hands in his jeans pockets, hunching his shoulders as he glanced at the floor. "It wasn't like we were engaged then."

"You were in a relationship, you jerk. If Bree found out,

do you think she'd say, 'oh well, it was before he proposed?' Hell no."

"I don't intend for her to find out."

Should he tell Alan about Holly? So far, he'd kept her out of it, dodging the man's frantic questions regarding how Luke had learned of Alan's indiscretion. The situation made Luke sick to his stomach, as it resurrected the hellish time of Sara's betrayal. And he hadn't been anywhere close to proposing to her.

A mistake on Alan's part wouldn't destroy their fifteen years of friendship, but Luke's sympathies sided with Bree. "You may not have a choice about her finding out. The truth has a way of pushing to the surface, no matter how deep you try to bury it."

Alan's eyes widened. "You're not going to tell her, are you? I mean, it was a one-time thing. See, Bree had come to Stilton for the holidays already, and didn't have lunch plans. My lunch appointment cancelled on me. We walked out for lunch together. And, well." Alan shrugged. "You know how these things happen."

Luke barely kept his mouth from dropping open. Had it been that easy for Alan to forget his commitment to Bree? "No, I *don't* know how this happens. I know that lunch plans get cancelled. I know that another woman can be attractive and that flirting can be fun. But that's where my understanding of this whole thing ends. There's a line you don't step over, buddy." Luke clapped Alan on the shoulder, leaning down harder than required to make his point. "You keep it all in your head. Better yet, keep it in your pants."

"It turned out to be a positive thing. Being with LaTisha made me realize how much I love Bree." Alan looked toward the closed door, either lost in remembrances or trying to form words. "The sex was, like, empty with LaTisha. I mean, it was great, you know, because it was sex, after all, but I didn't feel happy afterward. Not like I do with Bree."

Luke couldn't believe the words coming from his friend's mouth. Alan had risked a loving relationship for "empty but great" sex? What did that even mean? How could Alan have expected to feel satisfied afterward? To feel like he did when he'd made love with Bree? "That's called guilt."

"No, I don't think that was it."

Luke despaired for his friend.

"It was more like 'okay, that's over.' Like a checked off box on a To Do list. I didn't want to stay in bed anymore or talk about our plans for the day. Of course, we didn't have any. It was, like, just hollow."

Because Alan was, like, just shallow. Luke sighed. "What now?"

Alan looked at him, genuine puzzlement on his face. "What do you mean, what now? Now, we get ready for the dinner, have the rehearsal and go out for my bachelor party."

"I'm not taking you anywhere."

"What?" Alan glared at him. "You're the best man. It's tradition."

"You had your last wild fling already."

"Oh. Okay, whatever."

"And you're not going out tonight without me. Just forget it."

"You don't get to decide what I can or cannot do."

Luke raised an eyebrow and stared him down.

Alan scowled. "Anyway, tomorrow I end up married to Bree. I know what I want. Her. And she never has to find out about LaTisha."

"I don't think that's the way it's going to happen."

Alan's jaw dropped. "You'd tell her?"

"Not me." Luke owed his friend a warning at least. "Holly."

"Aw, hell."

Holly didn't see him coming. She would haven't have had time to duck out of the Kennedys' back door anyway, so she mentally girded her loins when Bree's mom announced Alan's arrival. She'd done some hard thinking in the few hours since she'd told Luke about her mission.

He'd made compelling points. Would Bree be better off

not knowing? In these circumstances, Holly would want to know. She'd call off her own wedding to a cheater. And she'd feel doubly deceived if her friend knew about her prospective groom's infidelity and didn't tell her.

But as close as they were, Bree might feel the polar opposite. Even if Alan never cheated again--which Holly doubted--Bree would live a life of doubt and suspicion. What kind of marriage could they have if she could never fully trust him?

Mrs. Kennedy opened the door and hugged him. "We didn't expect to see you until later. What a pleasant surprise."

From the look on Alan's face, he knew Holly had caught sight of him at the Palmer House. He had a frown line between his brown eyes. Streaks of style gel stiffened his short, nearly-black hair where he--or the wind--had ruffled it out of order. He held his lanky body rigid with tension.

Damn Luke. He supported his friend by telling him but cautioned her against doing the same. She would fight for Bree's happiness, no matter how much she hated confrontation.

"Seeing you is always pleasant, Anne." His gaze moved to Holly. And hardened. "Holly. Glad you could make it in for Bree's special moment."

"A wedding is more than a moment." Holly showed her teeth in a smile that fooled Bree's mom. "A moment is something that passes. A wedding builds toward the future."

"It's the foundation," Mrs. Kennedy said.

"I think love is the foundation." Holly held his gaze. "Trust. Loyalty. Honor. Truth."

Alan glared at her.

"You're right, honey." Bree's mom gestured them to sit.

Holly took a seat across from him.

"Bree's not here yet, Alan," Anne said. "Holly and I were just baking cookies while we waited for her. Would you care for some?"

"That would be great. It smells great in here."

"Great," Holly emphasized with enough snark to make his face redden. "I'll get them for you."

She hurried off to the kitchen, planted her back to a wall, and took a deep breath. If only Bree's mom would step out on an errand. Confronting Alan the Cheater with her in the living room was impossible, which he well knew.

She'd love to have Anne Kennedy's support. As Bree's mother, she'd be a formidable ally, but Holly couldn't tell her until she'd told Bree. Then it would be Bree's choice what to do and whom to share the news with. Bree would have to give some explanation for cancelling the wedding. If that's what she chose.

Holly would tell her the truth and expose Alan for the cheater he was. She hoped the cancelled wedding wouldn't cause too much gossip. That could lead to questions or recriminations from the townsfolk along the lines of "if Bree had kept Alan happy, he wouldn't have strayed," and other such nonsense. Stilton had its charm, but it was still a small town. Both Bree and Alan had been away for years. Who knew what support the betrayed bride would get here? Fortunately, Bree could escape right after Christmas, returning to her job in Chicago.

Holly took three cookies in on a napkin and set them on a table so she wouldn't have to touch him. It galled her to serve him but she enjoyed a tiny revenge in hearing him have to thank her in front of Bree's mom.

"I wish you had time for a proper honeymoon," Mrs. Kennedy said, "especially since Bree has almost a week before school starts up again. We'd love to send you someplace warm and tropical."

"That sounds great." Alan clenched his teeth at the overused word. "I mean, warm. Especially when compared with going back to Chicago."

Holly snapped her fingers. "You could at least have a special night together. Have you ever stayed at the Palmer House?"

Alan choked on his cookie, coughing and gagging as he tried not to spit it out. Holly put on an expression of concern.

Mrs. Kennedy thumped his back several times before pulling her hand away. "Oh, shoot. I know you're not supposed to whack a person this way. Sorry, Alan. Old habit."

"That's...okay," he managed between coughs.

"Something hard to swallow?" Holly asked sweetly. *Like guilt, you cheating rat bastard?*

He wiped his mouth with the napkin. "I'm fine. Must have been a nut. Nothing wrong with the cookie. It was gr--good. You'll have to give Bree your recipe, Anne."

"She has it. Bree was always a good cook when she took the time."

"Bree has a lot of admirable qualities," Holly said.

Alan set his teeth. "I know that."

Mrs. Kennedy glanced between them. "Is there something going on?"

"No," Alan said.

"Now, you two better get along," Mrs. Kennedy admonished as though they were mischievous Pekingese pups trying to eat out of the same bowl. "You're both important to Bree and nothing will change that. Holly, you'll still be her best friend, even though she and Alan will form a new unit."

"I look forward to it," Alan said. "Being one with Bree in all things."

Was he saying he wouldn't cheat again? Holly wondered. Or that he thought Bree would side with him against her?

"And Alan," Mrs. Kennedy continued, "you have to accept Bree's friends. They'll still be important to her even after you're married. Holly most of all, since they've been friends for so long."

"For-ev-er." Holly grinned at Bree's mom as she quoted *The Sandlot,* a movie she and Bree had watched all of one summer, almost on auto-replay. "Nothing could come between us. And, of course, I'll be more than thrilled for her when she marries a loving man who puts her first in all things."

She smiled, which appeased Bree's mom, but Alan understood she didn't refer to him.

He glared at her.

If he wasn't careful, his face would freeze that way.

CHAPTER SIX

Tension drained Holly's energy reserves until she thought she might drop from sheer anxiety. All day she'd sought an opportunity to talk to Bree without success. The exasperating woman hadn't shown in time for Holly's fitting, which Holly had wanted to skip. What was the point when the wedding probably wouldn't take place the next afternoon, if ever? And if it did, would Bree still want Holly to stand for her?

Mrs. Kennedy insisted, and Holly couldn't give her a good reason to duck out of it. So Holly donned the pink and gray swirled skirt with its gray satin tank top and pink jacket, which fit well enough with a tuck or two.

Bree had excellent taste, knew Holly's size from countless shopping trips together, and knew what would flatter Holly's coloring. As a third grade teacher, Bree dressed in clothes she could wear outside for recess or to sit on the floor. In her free time, she let loose her inner fashion diva. Had this been a happier occasion, Holly would have worn the outfit again. It was truly lovely. As things stood, however, she would donate it as soon as she returned to the city.

Waiting chewed at her nerves, even as she kept busy helping Bree's mom bake for the wedding guests and the holiday. She'd checked into the Stilton Inn that morning, not sure where she stood with Luke, and not wanting to take advantage of his hospitality whichever way their feelings led. Bree arrived home just fifteen minutes before the dinner party with her other bridesmaid, her cousin Marie, in tow.

Holly and Bree had time for hugs before Bree ran upstairs, supposedly to the restroom. She returned already dressed for the dinner, and Holly missed the opportunity to talk while Bree changed. A sparkling coral dress that bared Bree's shoulders set off the shimmer of her upswept blond hair. Killer taupe, three inch heels showcased her legs. She appeared the radiant bride-to-be. It broke Holly's heart to think of shattering that happiness.

Holly had also pulled her hair up for the evening, although she didn't feel much like celebrating. The simple navy dress she wore to presentations at work hovered on the line between classic elegance and funeral garb, making it fit for the night's occasion. As she and the vivacious Bree stood alone in a quiet moment now at the restaurant, few would suspect they had anything in common.

Holiday decorations graced Romero's Italian Restaurant,

but it retained its cozy Old World feel. The guests mingled in the large area outside the banquet room. Drinks were served, and Holly gratefully grabbed a sangria with extra fruit. She'd missed lunch and needed a vitamin C energy boost. Or maybe that came from the wine.

Stress had her wrung out. "I need a nap."

Bree glanced from Holly to Luke across the banquet room and back to study Holly's expression. "Is that code for something?"

"It means I didn't get much sleep last night."

"Oh." Bree looked at Luke again, then back, a frown forming between her eyebrows. "Okay, so, is *that* code for you had sex with Luke?"

Holly's eyes widened with embarrassment. Someone could overhear. She glanced around, relieved no one stood nearby. "No, and lower your voice."

"Don't take out your sexual frustration on me. Go grab him and work it off or something. The girls around here say he's dynamite in bed." Her laugh came out high enough Holly wondered if Bree could be tipsy. "I don't want a grumpy bridesmaid."

At times like these, Holly questioned if she and her friend spoke the same language. "Not everything is about sex, Bree."

"Too bad for you." Bree showed her teeth in a bright smile, a little forced around the edges, and took off to greet a new arrival.

Holly bolstered herself with three deep breaths and a swallow of alcohol.

"Don't do it."

She twirled to find Alan the Cheater behind her, a look of panic on his face. Or maybe anguish? He had reason to feel both.

"You should have said that to yourself a few days ago. Then listened."

"I realized something from doing it, Holly. Bree is my future. She's too important to screw around on, and, anyway, I don't want to. I've sown my wild oats--whatever that means. I'm going to be faithful to her after we're married."

Holly glanced around the room and located Bree on the far side. No one stood near enough to Holly and Alan to overhear, but she found Luke's gaze on her. She set her teeth. She wouldn't let her best friend walk blindly down the aisle, no matter if Luke called it interfering or gossiping.

She was confused why he'd take Alan's side, despite their long-standing friendship. Luke had broken up with his last girlfriend because she cheated on him. So why was it all right for Alan to betray Bree?

"I can't take that chance," Holly said. "Once a cheater..."

Alan narrowed his eyes, the brown stare menacing as his face set into hard lines. This would be the face defendants saw in court. It made her uneasy. "Don't cross me, Holly. You won't like the outcome."

Surprise held her still. She'd known him for nine years, not counting their childhood where he'd been in her classes, though not really a friend. She would have said she knew him well. They'd double-dated on occasion, and he'd welcomed her as a third wheel too many times to count. A stranger stood before her now. Perhaps he meant it as a joke. She gave a light laugh, hearing its false notes. "Are you threatening me?"

"It's no threat."

She watched, flabbergasted, as he walked toward the bar. Did he mean it wasn't a threat or that, as the phrase went, it was a promise?

"What's going on?"

Holly jumped even as she recognized Luke's voice at her side.

"Darn it, Holly, what's the matter with you?"

"Sorry. Just don't sneak up on me, okay? That's the second time someone has come on me unawares." And your best friend just threatened me. Maybe. And kind of non-specifically. What would Alan do anyway? She laughed it off. "Never mind. I'm just nervous."

"Have you told Bree yet?" Luke looked around the room. "I don't see her. Is she in the back room crying?"

Holly shot him a dry look, not appreciating his smart

remark, especially as he must have seen Bree sometime during the evening. "She was over by the door greeting guests two minutes ago. If she was crying, I wouldn't be out here partying. So, no, I haven't told her yet."

"Good. Don't."

"Luke, I just don't understand you. How can you ignore his cheating?"

He took her elbow and steered her to a deserted corner. She yanked her arm from his grasp, not liking to be manhandled or shushed. Not that she'd intended to announce to all the guests that Alan the Cheater was a worthless slime ball. She'd let Bree do that. "Don't bully me."

"I'm saving you from embarrassing yourself."

She glared at him, fed up. "Don't do me any favors. I'm sick and tired of people telling me something's for my own good. You don't get to decide that."

"I don't know what you're talking about, but it must be some hang-up you're dragging here from Chicago."

He'd zeroed in on it, of course. Her supervisor thought she needed to stay in her position for another year to "learn" the company's way and had promoted a less competent male coworker instead. Her last steady boyfriend, many months before, had always chosen her wine and usually her dinner, insisting he was taking care of her, when in truth, he was being high-handed and insulting.

"Sorry," she said, to be fair. She recognized that she reacted stronger to Luke's maneuver because of those experiences, and he didn't deserve such a strong response. "Just don't drag me off against my will. Or try to shut me up."

"If that's how you see it, then I'm sorry." Luke ran a finger from her temple to her chin. "I sensed you were about to blow the pot off the beans, and I know you want to tell Bree before anyone else heard."

"So it was for my own good." She huffed out a breath. "Thanks for the attempt, but rest assured, I wasn't going to make a scene."

"Hey, go ahead and make a scene if you want." He grinned. "Grab me and kiss me till my knees give out."

She smiled reluctantly.

"I'll even pretend to let you dip me."

Holly shook her head at his silliness. "Not the time or place."

"That sounds promising. Are you thinking of another time and another place?"

She eyed him. "I thought you were mad at me for needing to tell Bree?"

"I disagree with you, Holly, but I understand why you're doing it." He took her hand. "It's none of our business."

"I disagree. She's my best friend. Not telling her would betray our friendship." She frowned. "Don't you wish someone had told you about your girlfriend's shenanigans?"

"Someone tried to tell me, but I already knew. It needed to play out like it did. I would have been suspicious of the motives behind anyone telling me."

"What do you mean?"

"If someone told me--"

"Your best friend," she reminded him.

"Okay. If my supposed best friend had clued me in, I would've wondered why he'd want to tell me something so devastating. Most guys don't enjoy talking about feelings and crap. I would wonder if he'd slept with her or if he wanted to. Was he confessing or protecting himself from being discovered?"

She frowned. "Why would you assume any friend--except Alan--had done something like that?"

His slight smile indicated he'd caught her dig at Alan. "Because I would have been hurt and lashing out. Betrayed and doubting everyone's actions."

"Really?" She hadn't thought of it like that. "I guess I can see how that might happen, at first. But, later, when you accepted it, wouldn't you have been glad you weren't being fooled any longer? That your friend had stopped you from being further hurt and embarrassed?"

He shook his head. "I had to wake up and smell the coffee like you did this morning, coming around in my own time as to what to do. You came for pancakes when you were ready. Let Bree make her own decision if--or when--she has to."

"This isn't breakfast, Luke. She's about to *marry* him."

He glanced around, presumably making sure no one had come close enough to overhear. "And Alan may have learned his lesson and become a better partner because of it. We don't know how this will develop."

"So I'm supposed to watch a train wreck when I could have thrown the switch and saved all those people?"

He put his arm around her shoulders. "I know you want to do the right thing, Holly. You've got a strong streak of honor. That's what we all love about you. But maybe the trains will pass on a side rail without incident, and you would have created a panic for nothing."

It didn't sit well that he might have a valid point because it made her doubt what she meant to do. She still wanted to save her friend future heartbreak, but she wondered if Bree would appreciate the gesture for what it was. Holly fell far behind Luke when it came to applying logic to a relationship. She was all emotion, the strongest right now being protection.

Although, if Luke were right, maybe telling Bree wasn't the wisest thing to do. Maybe Alan would be a stellar husband, and Holly would only destroy their trust. She recalled his parting shot, which, in all fairness, could have been made out of frustration with nothing behind it. "Have you ever thought

Alan had a mean streak?"

His eyebrows rose in surprise. "Not even once. Why do you ask?"

"No reason."

"Holly, you can't just throw something like that out there and let it hang. What's up?"

"He threatened me about telling Bree."

Luke stared. When he lifted a brow, she realized he still expected some big revelation.

"That's it," she said. That was enough. Should be, anyway.

"Threatened you with what?"

"Nothing in particular."

"Just 'don't tell Bree?' What did you expect, that he'd be thrilled? Encourage you to blab about his indiscretion?"

Anne Kennedy walked toward them, so Holly put a smile on her face, despite her irritation with Luke.

"Don't you two make the *cutest* couple?" Bree's mom enthused a little too loudly, wildly misreading their reason for standing close together and away from the crowd.

"We aren't a couple," Holly countered. How could she trust his moral code? Had he even talked to Alan? Had he tried to discover the truth of the situation? No, he didn't want any part of it. She could understand his aversion to nosing into Alan's business, but the situation outweighed that concern.

He should also consider maybe Alan wanted to get out of

the wedding. Perhaps he needed a friend to say "you don't have to do this if you're not ready." Wasn't Luke shirking his duties as best man and best friend by not acting?

"You don't have to hide your 'elationship from me, honey." Mrs. Kennedy slapped her arm playfully, the sting dulled by Holly's sleeve. Alcohol fumes wafted toward Holly. "I've known you both for years. You're perfect together. And you share all that past." She tipped back her glass, finishing the contents. "You were the most obdorable friends."

Holly smiled. *Obdorable?* They'd been adorable. They'd been horrible. They might even have been objectionable and obnoxious at times. She wasn't sure which descriptor Mrs. Kennedy meant.

"I aways thought," the woman continued, swaying a bit, "if you hadn't moved, you two would have been married right out of high school."

The woman must be mostly inebriated, if not out and out drunk. Holly glanced at Luke, who wore an indulgent smile. He nodded at Holly and made a motion with his hand as though bringing a glass to his mouth, agreeing with her assessment. It hurt that they could be so in tune on some things and so out of sync on another.

"Let's find you a chair," Holly said.

Luke left, presumably to bring one to them.

"Tha's what makes Bree and Alan so perfect, you know?"

Mrs. Kennedy said. "They grew up together. They went to college together. They know each other's favorite desserts, as well as their bad habits."

Holly grimaced. Bree didn't know of *all* Alan's bad habits.

Or did she? Would Alan's cheating come as a surprise? Holly reviewed what she knew of their relationship. She'd been beside them since college, and she and Bree talked about everything, including sex. Bree had come to her several times after fighting with Alan, but she'd never once given any indication he'd even flirted with another woman, let alone cheated.

Luke returned dragging two chairs.

"You are too sweet." Mrs. Kennedy sank onto one, a little off-center before correcting her position. Holly sat beside her, the better to catch her.

"Anything for you, Anne," Luke said.

"How about another martini, then, young man? Gin."

With a shrug for Holly, he turned and left again.

"Mrs. Kennedy, maybe you should have some juice or water. Alcohol is dehydrating."

The older woman laughed. "Where did you hear that? In Chicago?" She patted Holly's cheek a few times, probably a little harder than she intended. "Call me Anne, honey. You're a grownup now."

Holly rubbed her cheek, glad Anne's aim had been slightly

off and she'd mostly hit cheekbone rather than tender flesh. "Anne." She smiled. "I'm going to have some water. When Luke gets back, why don't I get us both a nice cold glass?"

This, at least, she could do for Bree--keep her mother from being hung over the day of the wedding. Bree might need her mother later for consolation. Or to hire a hit man. "You don't want to be out of commission if Bree needs you."

"She doesn't need me." Anne's face crumpled as her body sagged. Holly grabbed her arm to keep her from slipping to the floor, but Anne pulled away and righted herself. "My little Aubrey's all grown up too and getting married. She'll have her own family now."

"That's how life should be," Holly said, hoping Anne wouldn't burst into singing *The Circle of Life*, "but it doesn't mean she won't need you. Especially these next few days."

Anne took a moment to focus then stared at her. "What?"

"A bride needs her mother." Holly couldn't say more now.

"Tha's not true of my Bree. She's strong. Self-surprising." Anne frowned. "That's not the right word. Self-fishing? No, tha's just silly."

"Self-sufficient?"

"Tha's it." Anne slapped Holly's arm with gaiety. "You're so smart."

Any more praise from Mrs. Kennedy and she'd need an ice pack. "Look, let me get us some water, and we'll see if Luke can snag us a couple of appetizers." *To soak up this alcohol.* Sitting down hadn't been the greatest idea. Holly had barely eaten all day. Tension, tiredness, and lack of food combined to knock her out. The sangria hadn't helped.

"Is a nice party." Anne glanced around the guests. "I a'ways liked this place."

Holly shot her a glance as her slurring worsened. "Come here often?"

"When we seller-brate something," Anne said with care, perhaps recognizing her intoxicated state. "I like the feted-chini."

"Yes, I've heard it's good."

Anne leaned closer and wound up with her head on Holly's shoulder. "And get the house dressing. Is wonerful."

Luke returned with a cup and another chair. "I'm sorry, Anne, they were out of gin so I got you this."

Anne took the cup and sipped. Her nose wrinkled. "It tastes like coffee."

"That's what I've heard." He winked at Holly.

Holly mouthed "thank you" as Anne drank. Coffee might work better than water, but she also needed to get some food into Bree's mom. Into herself as well, before she fainted from hunger. "Do you think you can find us some crackers? I'm starving."

He frowned at her then looked at Anne. "Are you? Well,

then, I need to do something about that."

"Wait." Holly felt awful for sending him on errands, but she needed to stay and hold Anne steady on her chair. Walking might have become a problem. She couldn't spot Bree, who she would have flagged to try to get the meal started. A glance at her watch indicated another fifteen minutes before the meal started.

She turned to Luke. "Maybe if we sat in the dining room, we could get some brought to us there? And we could weave our way in there now without alerting the crowd." She winked at Anne. "Get the best seats."

"I think we're s'pose to sit at the head table."

Luke bowed and crooked his arm toward her. "May I take you in, madam?"

Anne giggled and Holly grabbed her tilting coffee cup. Anne latched on to Luke's arm with enough force to make him wince. He turned to Holly and held out his other arm. "I'll escort you both."

Grateful, she nodded. "You're such a gentleman."

"At times." The wicked gleam in his eyes suggested occasions he wasn't at all restrained.

A shiver of awareness trailed down Holly's back. *Stop it.* She wasn't likely to be on the receiving end when he deliciously forgot his manners. When he took what he wanted. When he didn't ask permission.

Her breathing quickened. She swallowed hard. Wasn't going to happen, she reminded herself. Fidelity, a sacred topic for her, was a gray area for him.

The crowd trickled into the dining room behind them, taking Anne's move as a cue. No one seemed to notice the lady's occasional sideways step.

"You seem to have your hands full," a male voice said behind Luke.

They turned carefully to find Bree's dad, Doug, smiling knowingly.

"It's my pleasure," Luke said.

"Well, one of them is mine," Doug said, "and I've come to claim her."

Anne giggled.

Doug shook his head. "Just as I thought."

"What?" Anne asked.

"You're infatuated with the boy." But Doug's nod to Luke indicated gratitude for caring for her.

"He's taken," Anne said.

Doug eased her into an upholstered chair and pushed it up to the table. He glanced at Holly and Luke. "Really? I hadn't heard."

"Heard what?" Anne asked.

Doug placed a hand on her shoulder to help her swaying form stay upright. "Wedding bells?"

"No, it's not like that," Holly said at the same time Luke said, "No, it's too soon for that."

She jolted, wondering if she'd heard right. *Too soon?*

"I mean." He shrugged, sheepish. "We're just getting reacquainted."

Doug grinned. "Boy, your goose is cooked."

"Not yet," Luke said. "At least give me until Christmas."

The older couple laughed. Holly swallowed hard and set the cup on the table, rattling it only slightly. "Is there more coffee and maybe some crackers?"

"Good idea." Doug glanced around. "I'll find a waiter."

"I can do that, sir." Luke hurried off, leaving Holly to wonder if he was embarrassed by either Doug's suggestion or his own answer.

Too soon. She'd have to mull that over later. Maybe she'd read more into it than Luke intended.

"You're at the head table with Bree," Anne said.

"I've got things covered here," Doug assured Holly.

"What things?" Anne asked.

"You, my sweet." He leaned over and kissed her forehead.

Was he being discreet in public or did the paternal kiss indicate the dynamics of their relationship? In thirty years, would Holly's future husband give her a peck on the head and call it good? Doug meant it as affection rather than dismissal, she knew. Anne barely staying on her chair might be a deterrent to affection as well. Holly tried to convince herself of the merits of contentment as she slid into a chair at the adjacent table.

Luke set crackers in front of Anne, said something to her and Doug, then slid in beside Holly, handing her a pack of saltines. "They're bringing coffee."

"That's a relief." She tore into the cellophane. "Thanks for taking care of it."

He smirked. "A little fuzzy headed, are you?"

"Maybe a little. I didn't eat, unless you count three cookies." She caught his smirk. "Hey, they came out of the oven calling my name. You'd have done the same, buddy."

"I wish I could have. My cookies come pre-packaged from the store."

She laughed. "You own an oven."

"I'm not a baker. I make a mean pot of stew and of course, fireman's chili. I'm a master at grilling steak and half-decent at gumbo."

"Half-decent gumbo? Sounds nauseating."

Luke shook his head. "Smarty. When do you plan to talk to Bree?"

"No time now and the rehearsal might be problematic. It'll have to wait till later tonight. I'll head over to her parents' house after the rehearsal."

"I wish you wouldn't."

"I know." She turned to thank the waiter as he set coffee

before her. "I have to, though. It would betray our friendship not to. We trust each other."

"She might get mad at you for interfering. Just because you think you'd want to know, Holly, doesn't mean everyone feels the same."

She speared him with a glance. "Just because you think you wouldn't have wanted to be told before finding out, Luke, doesn't mean everyone feels the same. How did you learn about it, anyway?"

He frowned. "This is hardly the time or place to discuss that."

Would Luke still be with his last girlfriend if she'd remained faithful? Even married? Did he regret knowing she'd cheated because it ended their relationship? Maybe it was better to live in blissful ignorance. She didn't believe that, but she had to take it into account when deciding what to tell Bree. She finished the coffee and crackers and felt marginally better.

Luke greeted the person pulling out a chair on his other side, which turned out to be Alan's dad, Tony, who'd come alone. Alan's mom, Lorraine, sat beside Bree's parents with her second husband.

Holly did pity Alan on that score. His dad had been a severe alcoholic, who turned melancholic rather than physically abusive. His depression had bled into other areas of his life, until Tony changed from the most adorable teddy bear of a man to an unreachable stone. Bree had related the tragedy to Holly when Alan's mother left Tony shortly after Alan entered college. Alan had become more focused, almost driven, earning his degree and going on to law school, driving out his own demons with hard work. Bree had stood by his side, his rock of normality, while she obtained her teaching degree.

Bree had seen him through some dark times. Maybe they'd weather this, as well. Holly groaned silently. Not being able to predict the future hobbled her now.

She eyed Alan the Cheater as he pulled out Bree's chair on the other side of Holly. Their gazes met, and an unattractive scowl crossed his face. Would he remain faithful? Could she stay in their lives with this secret between her and Alan? It would eventually wedge between her and Bree too. Holly would continually be watching him for signs of infidelity. It would reflect in their interactions, which would affect Bree.

If Bree knew the truth, wouldn't she always be suspicious of him too? That would be an ugly addition to their relationship.

Holly took a deep breath and admitted the truth to herself. If Alan never strayed, perhaps Bree would be happier not knowing. There. Luke might be right about that. However, she couldn't guarantee Alan the Cheater wouldn't live up--or down--to his new nickname. The not knowing ate at her.

"Thank you all for coming," Alan said, standing at his chair. "Please come find a seat. Dinner will begin in a few minutes."

Bree beamed up at him. She looked besotted, but with love, not alcohol.

The rest of the thirty or so guests took their seats. Waiters poured wine, although Holly put a hand over her glass, smiling as Tony did the same when the waiter appeared at his side. Tony winked at her, a happier man than she'd ever known him to be.

A salad slid in front of her, and she attacked it as though it might run away. The accompanying roll with butter would provide her with some quick carbs. Combined with the crackers and caffeine, she just might make it through the dinner and rehearsal without falling on her face.

"This is good salad," Bree said. "I love this place."

Holly swallowed, inhaling food like a starving teenager at a banquet. "It's lucky they had an opening here. Being the last weekend before Christmas, I'd have thought it would be booked for a party."

Bree leaned closer. "It was." She kept her voice so low, Holly could barely make out the words. "Alan's stepdad, Jim, paid the owner to move the other party to the little room in the back."

"Oh, no. That's awful. They shouldn't have to cram in somewhere since they booked the room first."

"No." Bree waved off her comment. "It's fine. They had a

smaller party so it'll be cozier back there for them. We wouldn't have all fit. And Jim bought them about ten bottles of champagne, which the restaurant is offering as though it came from them for the inconvenience. I'm sure they don't mind."

Holly frowned at Bree's nonchalance and turned back to the last of her salad. Jim buying off the restaurant seemed underhanded, the kind of thing Alan might have learned from him. She glanced at Jim, a normal looking man in a gray suit. Average height, not too fat or thin. If she saw him on the street, she wouldn't recall where she'd met him. Seated by the effervescent Lorraine in her leopard print, sequined dress, the stiff-backed Jim became nearly invisible.

In contrast, Tony was round, almost comic, with his tonsure of dark curly hair and red-veined nose. He laughed at something Bree's dad said, the loud guffaw drawing attention. Tony had rediscovered joy in his life. Jim looked like he'd never tasted it.

What lessons had Alan taken from each man?

Doug Kennedy stood, glass in hand. "While we wait for the entrees to be served, I'd like you all to raise a glass to this amazing young couple. Our Aubrey has always known what she wanted, and for most of her life, that's been Alan. He'll have to watch his step or she'll run him over."

"She already has," Alan called out.

A collective "aww" mixed with laughter.

Bree blushed as people tapped their wine glasses with their forks. Alan grinned wider and kissed her.

"That's enough of that," Doug admonished. "She's still my little girl."

"I'll always be your little girl," Bree said.

Again the crowd cooed their approval.

Doug cleared his throat. "That's right. So I'd like to propose a toast. Not to my baby, as you might expect, but to the man who was special enough and lucky enough to win her."

People cheered and drank.

Holly didn't move. No way could she swallow a mouthful of wine honoring Alan. Not yet. Not until things were settled.

"You're not drinking," Bree whispered. "Aren't you well?"

Darn. Holly hoped she'd pass undetected. Bree's expression held mild inquiry but no suspicion. Luke had stiffened behind Holly. She couldn't see Alan's face.

A tap came on her left arm. Luke's side. She turned to find Tony leaning across him.

"You can toast with water, you know." Tony smiled with understanding, indicating his glass of cola. He hadn't lowered his voice, and several people glanced their way. "There's no shame in having a problem, Holly."

Luke laughed but turned it into a cough. She wanted to kick him but knew Tony would sense the move.

"No, I'm fine. Really. But thanks."

"I'd be happy to talk with you later," Tony said. "I have a good sponsor if you need to talk to someone. It's always harder around the holidays so we have extra meetings. There's one tomorrow morning."

"I don't have a problem." Holly smiled through gritted teeth as Luke's body shook with his silent mirth. "But thank you."

Tony tsked. "No good comes out of denial, young lady, but I know better than anyone you can't be pushed into recovery."

Heads turned as Lorraine stood. Her curvaceous body leaned on her husband's as she lifted her glass. Dressed like a hormonal teenager seeking attention, she patted her newly blond hair into place.

Holly hoped she didn't fall out of the top of her dress.

Lorraine fixed her stare on Holly with a sharp smile. The room went silent. "Please lift your glasses of whatever you have to drink in a toast to my son on his good fortune."

Not all gazes turned to Holly, of course. Some fell away in discomfort. Holly revised her hope about the dress. It would serve Lorraine right to be as embarrassed as Holly. Her face flamed. Her hand lay unsteady on the table. She could pick up the glass and drink the water. She should just do it.

Bree nudged her. Luke's hand landed on her leg...in support? Which way did he want her to react? She could just pick up the glass.

"Holly?" Lorraine called her out like a bully on the playground.

She opened her mouth to change the toast. To hope for Bree's future happiness. Yes, that she could--

The fire alarm went off.

People jumped, half-rose, looked to see what others were doing.

From the corner of her eye, Holly saw Alan slide back onto his chair. He smiled at her, triumph on his face.

Holly gaped. Had he really just set off the fire alarm, fearing she'd expose his infidelity?

"I'm sure it's nothing," he said to the room at large. "But we should probably go out anyway. Maybe there's a fire in the kitchen."

That got people moving. Some grumbled about having to go outside without their coats. Others assisted the older guests.

Alan helped Bree to her feet and held out his arm to Holly. "Do you need a hand?"

Luke cupped her elbow. "I've got her."

Alan turned away from the edge in Luke's tone.

"Jackass," Luke muttered.

"You saw him, too?"

"Yeah, but I would've known he'd done it anyway. It's typical Alan behavior."

Holly and Luke let others shuffle past them. The restaurant staff ushered out the patrons even as sirens wailed in the distance.

"Dammit," Luke said. "He just doesn't think. People could panic. The team gets called here, volunteers rush from their homes, and at the same time, they might be needed at another location."

"It'll be over quickly," she assured him. "As soon as they discover it's a false alarm. Right?"

He muttered a few more epithets. Then sighed. "We better go. It'll look suspicious if we stay in here."

"The waiters are staying because we are." Holly walked along with him, catching up to the other stragglers who'd gone for their coats.

"I can't believe people sometimes," he said quietly. "Is it better to burn than be a little cold? To get in the way of the firefighters? To endanger the staff?"

"Not everyone thinks things through, Luke. This is likely a false alarm. People know that."

"Except for the time it's not going to be."

She patted his arm. "You're right."

He raised an eyebrow at her.

She grinned up at him.

"Are you placating me?" he asked.

"Are you being placated?"

"Wait till I get you alone."

"Yeah?"

His eyes darkened. "Yeah."

Even in the middle of an evacuation, her breath left her as she felt his pull on her senses. She'd clearly lost her mind. And she clearly didn't care as she asked, "What are you going to do?"

Her breathy tone didn't escape her notice--or his, judging by the way his nostrils flared with male interest. His fingers tightened on her elbow. She loved Flirtatious Luke.

"I," he said, "am going to..."

She waited, heartbeat caught in her throat as he leaned closer.

"Get out the chocolate fudge sauce."

"What?" Holly blinked.

"Warm it up a little," he continued in a low tone. "Wouldn't want it to burn anything tender."

"No. We wouldn't want that."

"Then."

"Yes?"

"I'm going to drizzle it over a banana."

She swallowed.

"And eat it in front of you. Not sharing."

She laughed, a little relieved, a little disappointed. "That's mean."

"I know you, Holly MacDonald." He waggled a finger at her. "I know what drives you crazy."

"You used to know me," she countered as they exited the outside door. "What makes you think I even like...chocolate covered bananas?"

"Get real."

She had to laugh. "Okay, truth is, I love them."

"Had you going, though, didn't I?"

Oh, yes, he had. He definitely had.

CHAPTER SEVEN

Luke spotted Alan outside the restaurant, shepherding people away from the building so the firefighters could get through. With his arm around Bree, Alan inclined his head toward them. Cool, but alert. Luke couldn't believe the gall of the man. Or yes, he could. That made it worse.

Luke led Holly over, hoping she wouldn't cause a scene. He could control his fury. He had no idea how Holly reacted in a rage. He eyed Alan. "You have no boundaries, do you?"

"What are you talking about?" Bree asked.

"It's nothing." Alan squeezed her close. "Luke's been listening to the wrong person. Now he's got his head turned around."

"Throwing the fire alarm is no joking matter, you jerk." Luke's hands curled into fists, as much at the insult to Holly as Alan's action. The jerk wouldn't care about people so Luke appealed to his selfish side. "If you get caught, you'll be fined and maybe have to serve one to three years in jail."

"Throw the fire alarm?" Bree chuckled. "He wouldn't do such a thing."

Alan stared him down, daring him to say something else. Luke tried to communicate the threat right back at Alan. *Don't push me, buddy.*

"You wouldn't do that, would you?" Bree asked Alan with a frown.

"Don't let him trying to quote the law scare you," Alan said to Bree. "I'd have to be convicted for any of that to happen."

Holly reached out to her with sorrow on her face. She was clearly not eager to have another of Alan's foolish actions exposed at the moment. Especially with thirty people glancing their way. "Let's leave the men to argue this out."

"I want to know what's going on." Bree stepped away from Alan and Holly. She glared at Luke. "I want to know why you think Alan would have disrupted our dinner like that. Or broken some law."

Luke's jaw clenched. "Ask him."

"Alan?"

"It's disorderly conduct, hon, and they're mistaken."

"You did get up during the toasts." Her brow creased.

"Well, I might have bumped it." Alan shrugged. "I don't know. I went to ask for a Coke for Holly, but I couldn't find a waitress so I sat down again."

"Oh, well, then." Bree turned to Holly and Luke, visibly

relaxing. "If he did it, which we don't know for sure, it was an accident."

"Most alarms don't trigger from a bump. But don't worry, the team will inspect the restaurant's systems to see if they had updated theirs. You should make a donation to the fire station." Luke pinned Alan with his gaze. "Just to show your gratitude for their quick response."

"I might do that."

"That would be nice," Bree said, "even though it might have been set off in the kitchen. They responded really promptly. We should ask Jim to donate, too, since the party was in his name. It would look good for his company."

Alan frowned. "Jim likes to keep a low profile. He's, like, shy or something."

"He's like, connected, or something," Luke muttered.

"What?" Holly asked with wide eyes.

"Well, he is from Chicago." Luke tried a smile. The man wasn't anywhere in sight. Hiding from the cops that had come with the firefighters?

Holly shook her head. "You need to get over this hangup you have about my home. It's 'My Kind of Town,' after all."

The three of them groaned at her mention of the classic Sinatra song, letting the jokes lighten the mood. Mission accomplished. At least Bree became distracted as she rushed to assure Holly that Alan's stepdad wasn't part of the mob.

Although that part wasn't a joke. If ever a man looked too normal and too bland, it was Jim Henry. Even his name sounded like a cover.

"Do you think they'll let us back in tonight?" Bree asked. "We have to feed all these people then get to the rehearsal."

"They should," Alan said. "If it's a false alarm, there's no reason we couldn't eat. Might even get a free bottle of champagne out of it."

Holly's jaw dropped.

Luke's tightened. "You're kidding, right?"

Alan shrugged. "I've been inconvenienced."

"Oh. My. God." Holly turned to Bree. "Can I talk to you for a minute?"

"No." Alan almost yelled it.

"Not now," Luke said. "Looks like people are heading back."

"Sorry for the bother, folks," Marty, a fireman Luke knew, called from the doorway. "We've given the all clear. There's no reason not to enjoy your dinner."

"Please-a," the manager called, waving his arms. "Come back-a inside. Everything, she is all right."

Luke laughed. "Did he just develop an accent?"

"Yeah, but I don't know where he's supposed to be from. Transylvania?"

"Italy, of course," Bree said. "This is Romero's Italian

Restaurant."

"Yes-a," Luke waved his arms in huge circles, imitating the manager. "I can-a see that-a now."

"Do you think that's his real accent and it's coming out under stress?" Holly wrinkled her brow as she considered. "Or is he putting it on--badly--for the audience? Trying to elicit pity so no one leaves?"

Alan frowned. "Who cares? Let's just go eat."

He hurried away, gripping Bree's arm.

"Would you really have told her just now?" Luke asked.

Holly blew out a breath. "I don't know. Probably not. Alan was ticking me off though."

"You certainly put the fear of Holly in him." Luke grinned. "Serves him right."

"I'm going to talk to her sometime tonight. Each time he opens his mouth, I'm overcome with the urge to have you punch him."

Luke laughed, feeling his tension fall away. He waved to a few of the guys from the fire station. "I might take you up on that. Alan and I haven't had a good brawl since we were about sixteen."

"Really? What did you fight over?"

"A girl, of course. About that time, I'd grown into control of my body instead of being awkward, rubbery limbs. Played varsity basketball."

"I didn't know that."

Luke shrugged. "No reason you would. Anyway, I finally found the nerve to ask a girl to the Homecoming dance. She'd accepted another offer already."

"Alan?"

"Yep. He'd asked her that morning."

"Did he know you wanted to ask her?"

"Yep. I'd told him the night before."

Holly winced. "Ouch."

"That's what he said."

They laughed as Luke held open the door. A few stragglers pushed in behind Holly. He had to admit, Alan didn't act like any kind of prize bridegroom. Luke still didn't agree that Holly should stick her nose into Bree's business, but he couldn't fault Holly's motives. The more he saw of her combined determination and reluctance, the more he appreciated her. She didn't want to break Bree's heart. Unlike Joanne Harkins who'd been only too eager to tell him about Sara's infidelity.

Luke pulled his chair up to the table. Joanne had shown the proper amount of sorrow over the situation, but she'd been too quick to offer consolation. The experience soured him almost as much as Sara's cheating had. But he couldn't hold that against Holly, who at least thought she was doing the right thing. Whereas Joanne had been plowing the field for her own takeover, Holly had Bree's happiness in mind.

Alan stood, glass in hand. "Okay, let's try this again."

The guests laughed.

"Please raise your glasses to my beautiful fiancée." He turned to face Bree. "Aubrey Kennedy, you made me the happiest man on earth when you accepted my proposal. There's nothing I wouldn't do, no obstacle I wouldn't face, to make you happy in return."

Luke glanced at Holly's profile to see if she'd picked up on Alan's challenge. Her jaw flexed as though she ground her teeth together.

"My future is yours," Alan continued. "My happiness grows out of yours. I intend to be the husband you need. No one on this planet is good enough for you, but no one on this planet loves you more than I do."

He sipped from his glass while the crowd declared their approval and joined him. Sounds of "cheers" and "to Bree and Alan" filled the area.

Luke had to hand it to him. The guy had a way with words.

Alan made a point of leaning over Bree to Holly. "Does the maid of honor want to make a toast?"

Luke held his breath. He had to hand it to him. The guy had guts.

Holly stood and raised her glass of water. "To Bree and her never-ending happiness. May Alan succeed in his efforts to be almost-worthy."

The guests laughed while Alan made a pained face then bowed in Bree and Holly's direction. "I will do my best."

The rehearsal went off without a hitch. Holly bit her tongue often enough to bruise it. Luke's presence kept her sane, and the pastor's sense of humor regarding the unexpected wedding eased them through the awkward moments.

"I'm glad you two didn't run off to Vegas," Reverend Jacobs said. "Nothing wrong with their weddings, mind you, but a ceremony in the house of the Lord reminds us all of the sanctity of the union. It unites the community. The family and friends you invited will help see you through the struggles in your marriage. But that's just my opinion." He smiled. "And a preview of tomorrow's service."

"We're grateful you fit us into your schedule," Bree said.

"I wasn't doing much of anything on Sunday, anyway."

Everyone laughed. He had two services, plus preparing for the ones on Christmas Eve and Christmas Day. Fitting the wedding into the afternoon must have been a hassle.

Holly noticed Alan blocking any attempt for her to get Bree alone. He'd even stood just inside the dressing room while she and Bree inspected it, listening to their conversation.

"Can we cut out the part about anyone objecting to the marriage?" Alan smiled as they practiced standing at the altar. "I don't want to risk Bree coming to her senses."

Holly stared him down. She noticed Luke stiffen.

"We don't do that anymore," the Reverend said. "It's anti-climatic when no one comes forward, although it would be highly dramatic if someone did. Very *Jane Eyre*."

Holly had no intention of delaying until the last moment. She'd bring her concerns to Bree later that night.

Holly waited outside the Kennedys' in the Corolla until Alan left at 10:12 pm. She'd have preferred to be at the motel, snuggled in bed, but she'd put off this talk long enough. Not wanting to disrupt the household at that hour, she tapped lightly. Anne had already taken her fuzzy head to bed, and Doug followed suit after kissing Bree and giving her a tight, unself-conscious hug.

Bree flitted around the living room, her To Do list in hand, checking the presents she and Alan had opened and displayed on a folding table against a far wall almost out of the way. "I don't know how we're going to get these all home. Or where we'll put them once we're there." Bree sighed. "We're keeping Alan's apartment because it's bigger, but I'll miss mine being so handy to the El stop and the Jewel."

He wanted her to give up her apartment? "We need to talk."

"I thought people would just give us checks or gift cards since it was such short notice." Bree smiled. "I bet Aunt Sue is cursing me right now. She likes to finish all her shopping by the first Sunday in December so she doesn't have to go out with the mad hordes."

Holly stepped in front of her. "Bree, sit down. I have to talk to you."

"Sit?" Bree laughed, waving her notepad. "I can't. Do you have any idea how much I have to do yet for the wedding? You can forget beauty sleep. I'll probably look like a hag tomorrow."

Holly grabbed her arm, spinning her around. "Aubrey. Sit."

Bree blinked and sank onto the sofa. "I know it's serious when you use my given name."

Holly perched beside her, taking her hand.

"You're scaring me, Holly. What's going on? Are you sick? Is it your parents?"

"No, no. Sorry. No one's dying." Holly groaned. "I don't mean I'm sorry they're not. Crap." She took a breath. "Just let me say this, okay? You know how you left Chicago last weekend to come home for the holidays?"

A smile flitted across Bree's features. "Given that it was seven days ago, yeah. I remember."

Holly grimaced. Trying to ease into the setup made her sound lame. "Right. Well, Monday I went out for a late lunch. I walked back afterward because I felt so full. And I wanted to mull over ideas for that project at work I told you about."

"The one driving you crazy."

"Yes. I walked past the Palmer House." Remembering how she'd screwed up while telling Luke, Holly reorganized the events to tell it straight this time. "And I saw Alan."

Bree tipped her head. "O-kay."

"He was with another woman. Kissing her."

Bree jerked back, her face set in denial. "What?"

"I'm sorry," Holly rushed on. Now that she'd started, she wanted to be rid of the task. "I don't want to have to tell you this, but he *was* kissing her. It wasn't platonic or casual. They went into the hotel."

Bree sprang to her feet, backing away but keeping her eyes on Holly as though she were a wild animal about to leap. "I don't believe it."

"It's true."

"You're mistaken. Or just plain wrong."

"Bree, I wouldn't say it if I wasn't sure."

Bree held up her hands to ward off reality. "I'm sure you think you know what you saw, Holly, but Alan would never be unfaithful to me."

Holly kept quiet, giving her time to accept the possibility. Bree paced away, stood in front of the gift table, her rigid back to Holly.

After a few silent minutes, Holly retrieved glasses and wine from the kitchen. She didn't need any more alcohol, but

Bree might. And soon.

Bree remained in the same spot when Holly returned. Relieved that her friend hadn't thrown all the presents to the floor, Holly set the wine and glasses on the coffee table. She filled a glass for each of them, the chardonnay sparkling.

"Who was she?" Bree's monotone sounded lifeless, as though she'd become the statue she resembled.

"I don't know."

"How sure are you about the kiss? About its non-platonic nature?"

Holly swallowed. "Absolutely. I'm sorry."

Bree moaned, bringing her hand to her mouth.

Luke's warning about the bearer of bad news echoed in Holly's mind. What would she do without Bree's friendship? How long would it take for Bree to be with her and not think of this day?

Bree turned, face set, eyes flat.

Holly's insides chilled with her helplessness. She couldn't do anything to ease her friend's pain. She'd caused it. Okay, Alan held partial blame, but if Holly hadn't told her, Bree would still be anticipating her marriage. "I'm sorry."

Bree sat in the chair across from her, the chair Holly had taken earlier that day to face off with Alan. She sipped some wine, staring into middle-space. Into nothingness.

"I know I can't un-see it or un-say it," Holly said, "but is there anything I *can* do for you?"

"No."

The word hung stark.

Feeling uncomfortable and unwelcome, Holly wanted to leave, but she wouldn't go until Bree told her to. Until she...released her. They sat, wrapped in shared misery, apart as they'd never been.

Minutes stretched. Holly didn't touch the wine. She didn't deserve to take the edge off her misery. Luke had been right. This had been a mistake.

"I'm going to bed." Bree rose. "Lock up on your way out."

Holly watched her leave the room, wondering if their friendship would survive. At least Bree hadn't doubted her word, not after the first moments of impact passed.

Holly carried the wine to the kitchen and rinsed the glasses. She checked the deadbolt on the front door then left out the back, flipping the thumb lock behind her.

Her windshield had frosted over, the warm defroster granting Holly a minute to collect herself before heading out. She rubbed her hands together, feeling chilled all over. And so alone.

Reversing out of the Kennedys' driveway, she drove on instinct, the memory of Bree's emotionless face floating before her. Fortunately the streets were quiet, people tucked into their cozy homes. The short drive seemed endless. Holly just wanted to feel warm inside again.

She got out of the car and went across the walkway. The door opened.

"I told her."

Luke gathered her into his arms.

Luke held Holly close, the weight of her telling Bree impacting them both. He couldn't blame her for protecting her friend. He'd warned Alan that Holly knew, after all, so he'd basically done the same.

He led her to the couch where he sat with her draped across him. At least he could offer her a safe and quiet space. Despite not wanting her to ruin the wedding in the first place, Luke could only feel relieved that she'd turned to him. Trusted him not to berate her or say, "I told you so." He wanted to ask questions--had Bree confronted Alan? Was the wedding off? And most importantly, had Bree said something to devastate Holly? Or was this just sorrow and the release of tension? Instead, he only held her, letting her soak in the security he offered. His friendship that would never fade, despite years and distance.

Friendship. It would be enough. For now.

After several minutes, Holly looked up at him from where her head rested on his chest. "Thanks. I needed a friend."

"Always."

He didn't say more, didn't ask those questions. She snuggled in for another minute then straightened to sit beside him. He immediately missed her warmth, her scent, her trust.

Holly's hairclip had fallen out or been removed at some point, but she wore the dark blue dress from the dinner. She still looked elegant, if bruised around the eyes. Around her spirit.

"Coffee?" he suggested. "Hot chocolate?"

"I'm good, thanks. Maybe some water?"

He rose and returned with two iced glasses. She gulped half of hers.

"When I told Bree, she didn't say much." Holly stared into her glass. "She internalized it. It took a minute or two, but then she was unreachable. Frozen."

"I'm sorry."

"You were right. No--" Holly continued when he would have cut her off. "I should have minded my own business. She won't let me help her through this."

"Holly." He took her by the shoulders and waited until her gaze met his. "Do you think it was fair to let her marry Alan without knowing?"

"I don't know."

"Yes, you do. Think about your trip down here. Think about your reasons for telling her, even when I advised against it."

"You were right."

"I'm not so sure about that, and it isn't the point I'm making here. Did you believe you were doing the right thing for Bree?"

"Yes, but she's--"

"No buts. You did what you had to. Your friendship spurred you on to that decision."

"I guess."

He smiled. "You know it. Right or wrong, Holly, you acted out of love."

"I'm not sure Bree thinks that."

"Honey, Bree is reeling. She had two possible reactions to you telling her and she chose shutting down. For now."

Holly's sad expression broke his heart. "Do you think," she whispered, "Bree will ever forgive me? That we can be friends again?"

Luke hugged her and kissed the top of her head. "What makes you think you're not still friends?" He sent a brief mental plea to Bree. *Please don't abandon Holly.* "Let's see what tomorrow brings, okay?"

She shuddered in his embrace then nodded. "It's been a long day."

He thought back to them in the kitchen that morning. It seemed like a week had passed. "Yes, it has. Do you want to stay here again?"

She shook her head and straightened. "All my stuff is at the hotel."

"Better and better." His teasing coaxed a response at least.

"I don't think I'm up for that tonight. Sorry, buddy."

"I'll be here when you are."

She blinked.

He shrugged, wishing to pull the words back in his mouth. Dammit. Not a good time to make a pass at her. "I'm a guy. What can I say?"

Her relief should have insulted him, but he knew the kind of emotional tidal wave she'd ridden for the past several days. It surprised him she remained upright. "Let me drive you to the motel. I'll come get you in the morning or Micah and I will bring your car to you."

"That's too much bother."

"Honey, you're dead on your feet."

"True." She raised her shoes for inspection. "Almost literally. I spend too much time in heels."

"I have slippers. We could stuff the toes."

Finally, Holly laughed. "No, thanks. Fifteen more minutes in these won't kill me."

They bundled up for the short trip as the sky had cleared of clouds, letting all the Earth's heat escape into the atmosphere. Leaving her at the Stilton Inn, even waiting while she entered her room, contradicted every impulse fueling Luke at that moment. He could have held her all night, as a friend rather than a lover. Offering support, providing a shelter. But at least she'd come to him when she was hurt. That meant something. It would have to be enough.

What would tomorrow bring for him and Holly? For Alan and Bree?

He drove home, more alone than he'd ever felt. What a pansy, he thought, but he couldn't help wondering: If it hurt this much now to be without her, how would he survive when Holly left in three days?

CHAPTER EIGHT

December 23rd

Holly rose at five a.m., checking again for a missed call and to ensure her cell phone held a charge. She flipped on the light. Getting back to sleep was unlikely. She waited for Bree's call, wished for it, no matter the time, hoping her friend would forgive her.

After all, Holly had done the exact same thing that drove *her* crazy. She'd acted in Bree's "best interests." It had maddened Holly when her ex-boyfriend ordered her food. It maddened her when her boss promoted a less-qualified man ahead of her using that lame excuse. Now she'd probably maddened Bree.

When the motel phone rang, she jumped in surprise. Bree would call her cell phone, wouldn't she? Who else would call here? Her heart thumped with anxiety.

"I saw your light go on," Luke said after her breathless

hello. "I just drove past there."

Holly sagged with relief and disappointment. Not an emergency, but not Bree, either. "What are you doing out?"

"Thinking. Gassing up the truck. Did you sleep at all?"

"Some, I think. The sangria before dinner helped."

"I should have thought of that."

"You didn't sleep?" She curled onto the bed and leaned back against the pillows. The intimacy of the dark morning and Luke's voice in her ear combined to ease her tension. Her shoulders relaxed, followed by her back muscles. She sank into the mattress as her heartbeat slowed to a steady cadence.

"I dozed some, I think. Have you heard from Bree?"

"No. Have you heard from him?"

Luke's soft exhalation conveyed humor at her refusal to use Alan's name. "No. It's pretty early for most people."

She smiled. "Although you're usually up with the chickens?"

"No, fortunately. Trees grow without assistance." He went silent.

She didn't want to sever the connection, didn't want to be alone. She wouldn't sleep; she couldn't help Bree until she called. Luke's voice soothed her. Luke's understanding soothed her. "Are you going back to bed?"

"No point," he said.

"Then we might as well be together in our misery. Do you

know anywhere that serves breakfast at this ungodly hour?"

"Chez Luc?"

Holly laughed. God, that felt good. She hadn't known when she'd be able to smile again, let alone laugh out loud. The odd thing was it didn't feel too soon. With Luke, everything felt just right.

Being with Luke, even talking with him at a distance, brought her pleasure. That both warmed and disconcerted her. She had to return to Chicago and to work in two days. She had today--wedding or not, then Christmas Eve and Christmas Day left. She'd have to leave Christmas night at the latest to return the Corolla to her colleague. If Bree rejected her help, Holly might return home today. The only thing to keep her in Stilton other than Bree was Luke. Since their relationship fluttered in mid-air, she couldn't see the point of remaining.

Reality loomed, making her want to duck.

"I'll come pick you up," Luke said. "I know a place by the highway. Then we'll swing by my house so you can get your car."

Her heart lifted with anticipation. "Sounds like a plan. Give me half an hour to dress."

"Will do." He hung up.

Holly chided herself for being disappointed because he didn't suggest she waited to get dressed until after he arrived. She'd grown used to his teasing. But, she wondered as she grabbed clothes and headed for the shower, did his teasing go deeper than the mere flirtation of old friends? Would she leave with memories but nothing else? Or would she suggest a long-distance relationship and see what developed? After all, she could come to Stilton for a long weekend once or twice a month. If she bought a car. Or Luke could come visit her. Trees went dormant for the winter. Surely she and Luke would have a month or so to discover whether they had a future before the orchard needed him.

Scrubbing in shampoo more vigorously than necessary, Holly rejected that plan. No matter where they spent the next months together, the problem lay in their different lives. He couldn't move the Ivey Orchard or find work in his field, ha ha, in Chicago. The sacrifice would have to be hers.

It would be a sacrifice, too. She had to face it. Despite being passed over for that last promotion, she made strides toward becoming vice president every day. Her salary enabled her to live in a nice apartment and travel the world if she wanted. Life in Stilton, while charming, couldn't compare.

She threw on jeans and a sweater, banishing the worry. For the present, they didn't have romance between them. They shared a problem in their friends' wedding/non-wedding. She dried her hair and dabbed extra makeup under her eyes. When his knock sounded, she drew a deep breath and reminded herself, "just friends."

For now.

"You look great," he said after a hug. They hurried across the frigid parking lot and climbed in his blessedly warm truck. "No one looking at you would ever know you hadn't slept."

"Good." She flipped down the mirror on the visor as he reversed. She couldn't agree with his assessment, but at least she'd washed most of the haggardness from her features. "Where's this breakfast place?"

"It's a truck stop." He glanced at her. "You okay with that?"

Instead of rolling her eyes at him, she batted her lashes. "Sure. Can't wait. The pickin's are slim downtown for good truck stop food."

"At least you know there is such a thing as good truck stop food."

"We'll see. I have high standards."

The worried glance he gave her as he drove through the dark streets should have been amusing. Instead, it underlined their differences.

"Relax, Luke. I'm kidding."

"You're used to ethnic variety and haute cuisine."

"And burgers and hot dogs and fried chicken. I liked the Dew Drop In food. I'm sure this place can do up pancakes or omelets."

He smiled. "They're almost as good as my pancakes."

As it turned out, the food merited a rave review. Pancakes as fluffy as Luke's were made that much yummier with a topping of cinnamon honey butter. Crispy hickory-smoked bacon dipped in egg yolk made her stomach growl for more. The coffee rivaled any she'd bought in the city. At a quarter of the price. With free refills. She noted the exit number from the highway for her next visit to Stilton--which might occur sooner than she'd ever imagined if she and Luke pursued the potential of a romance.

The not-knowing drove her insane. How to broach the subject delicately?

Luke pushed away his empty plate. Bits of gravy-soaked biscuits lay beside the catsup and a tidbit of sausage and scrambled egg. "Okay, let's figure this out. Today, we either have a wedding at two or we spend the morning canceling it."

Holly set down her fork, disheartened by the reminder. "Right. I charged up my phone last night."

"That's pessimistic. Do you think she'll call it off?"

"What else can she do? At the least, it will be postponed. Bree will need time to adjust to knowing about his cheating."

Luke twirled his coffee cup, staring into the liquid. "She could forgive him and they could go through with the wedding."

"She could. I don't know why she would, but sure. If love has blinded her enough to Alan's dark side, she might. I just don't believe that will happen today."

He cocked an eyebrow. "You're not the forgiving type?"

"If you squeeze the toothpaste from the middle of the tube, I'll get over it." She set her plate on the side of the table for pick up. "Cheat on me and I'm gone."

"Good to know. I feel the same."

"So you wouldn't have forgiven your ex?"

He shook his head. "There wasn't any reason for her to sleep with anyone else if she loved me. She must not have, or not deeply enough."

Holly put her hand over his. "She was an idiot. You're well rid of her."

"I'm glad I'm not with her now." He smiled. "Being free opens me to possibilities."

"Such as?" She hoped he didn't notice her hand go moist atop his.

"Such as us, Holly. Let's stop dancing around it. I want to see if we have something more than childhood memories. What about you?"

The room went white. Only the deep blue of Luke's eyes shone against the void. All action around them faded. This was it, the moment she'd hoped for.

A chill swept over her as she tried to find her voice. "Will we still be friends if the romance part doesn't work?"

"I don't know. We'll have to see how it plays out. What do

you say?"

Saying yes would commit her to Luke. They'd start this weekend, being together as a couple through the coming ordeal, perhaps making love after the wedding situation got settled. They'd make time to commute to be together. If they could make it work, if they fell in love and stayed in love, this might be the last unattached moment in her life. From now on till death, she might be part of a couple. With Luke.

Goose bumps chased across her skin.

Was she willing to consider a future with him? Seventy years from now, would she still want to be a couple? Was the chance for his love worth possibly losing his friendship?

One word resounded in her chest. "Yes. I'd like to see where this could go."

His smile lit her heart. She relaxed as joy swept over her. Movement began again in her peripheral vision as colors returned.

"Me, too. Do you think anyone would notice if we sealed our agreement with a kiss?"

Her cheeks warmed. "Let's wait. No one wants to witness that kind of thing over breakfast."

"They'll think we're ending the evening."

"Having said that we should see where this goes--"

"No take backs," Luke interrupted.

"No. No take backs," she assured him. "But it would be

insensitive to flaunt our budding relationship when Bree is in trouble with hers."

"Alan probably won't notice, but you're right. Bree could be upset by it. We can keep it on the down low."

She laughed. "I love when you talk street. It sounds like a foreign language coming out of your mouth."

"What? I can be city smart."

Holly eyed his red and blue flannel shirt worn over a royal blue T. "Sure you can. But I like you the way you are."

"Thanks. I think." He grinned. "Let me pay for the meal then we'll head over to the Kennedys'."

She glanced at her cell phone. No missed calls or texts. "It's not quite six."

"We'll see if their lights are on. Doug has trouble sleeping, too."

"How do you know that?" She rose and gathered her things.

Luke helped her into her coat. "We sometimes wind up here at the truck stop together for breakfast. He runs in my neighborhood."

"Really?" She shook her head. "I can't help but be amazed at how you have your finger on the pulse of this town."

"Micah takes care of half."

"The female half?"

Luke paid the bill. "Ever the charmer, that's our Micah."

"Which is going to get him into trouble one day."

"I can't wait." He chuckled when she scowled at him. "Seriously. I want popcorn and a front row seat. That boy has it coming."

"So much for familial support."

"Wait. Where's your new hat?"

Holly grimaced and pulled the Scout leader's cap from her pocket. Luke raised his brow and waited while she donned it. "Stupid leader."

"It's from me. To keep your head warm." He kissed her cheek. "I'll keep your heart warm."

He held the door for her then slipped his hand around hers. Sheer anticipation burst forth in laughter. "I'm romancing Luke Ivey."

He grinned. "I'm being romanced?"

"You can romance me back."

"I'm romancing Holly MacDonald," Luke shouted to the parking lot, his breath frosting the air. "You're right. There's something surreal about it."

"Who'd a thunk, huh?"

"Not me. I barely even noticed you were a girl."

"Neither of us thought of the other like that."

He looked away.

Surprised, she tugged on his hand to halt him. "What? You did notice?"

"When we were ten going on eleven."

"I had no idea." She watched their breaths go white on the breeze.

"Thank God you didn't. I would have been horrified. Seeing my best friend in a new light appalled me."

"What changed?"

"My dad gave me the birds and the bees speech."

"Oh. My. Lord." She felt her face flame for her eleven-year-old self. "You and me and sex? Isn't that young?"

"Yeah, well, Dad didn't want to wait until too late. They teach it in school in third grade. I couldn't be with you without noticing our differences."

"Sheesh. I can't believe he did that. He could have wrecked our friendship."

"Hey, give the old man a break. I had just blown you up for the third time."

She laughed. "Oh, right. The food mixture experiment. That was ugly."

"Dad said I had to take care of you. I asked why." He shuddered dramatically. "It got weird from there."

"Girls aren't allowed to explode?"

"Men take care of their womenfolk."

"Oh, good grief. I'm surprised you ever knocked on my door again."

"I'm knocking now." He leaned in, slowly.

His lips brushed coldly against hers, but his kiss sent sparks through her veins.

"I'm glad I didn't explode you, Holly."

She laughed at his phrasing and could have told him she felt close to exploding right then. Given the fragility of their new relationship, she settled for, "I'm glad you didn't, either."

They weren't visible from the diner so Holly pulled him closer. "I've heard rumors about you, Luke Ivey. The girls all say you're dynamite in bed."

He closed his eyes and his cheeks darkened. "Well, this is awkward."

"I know, but is the rumor true?"

He snorted. "How can I answer that? What's in the past isn't relevant."

"I don't care how many... Okay, let me rephrase that." She didn't want to know and would never inquire. "I'm not asking about your past lovers, Luke. I just want to know, if you're such a dynamo, why we haven't...why you haven't...?" Her cheeks blazed with heat. Good thing she had a fireman in her arms.

A grinning fireman. "Holly, when the time is right, I'll let you decide for yourself how good I am. I'm looking forward to your opinion."

"Then why aren't you *doing* anything about it?"

He laughed at her petulance. "I figured you get enough of that kind of guy in the city. The guy in a hurry, making deals, climbing the corporate ladder. That's not me."

She gave a frustrated groan. "What does a guy's career ambitions have to do with how he makes love? More to the point, what does it have to do with you not putting a move on me?"

"A man's job influences his entire personality. I'm not looking for moves, Holly. I want a future." He kissed the tip of her cold nose.

"And in the meantime, I've been rushing at you like a nymphomaniac, trying to get a response."

"Yeah, you have." He grinned. "And it's been terrific."

"You like aggressive women?"

"I like you."

She laughed.

He beeped the truck's locks and helped her in. Once the door closed, she let out a short, soft squeal, celebrating being Luke's girlfriend, then shut it off as he neared his door.

"Did you say something?" he asked as he climbed inside.

"Nope."

"Are you good with going together or do you want to pick up your car first?"

She shook her head. "Let's just go there. If no one's up, we'll get my car."

He drove them to Bree's without much verbal exchange. Several times she stole a glance and found him darting his gaze her way. She smiled self-consciously then in shared delight at their situation. Few cars passed them. With the wispy fog hanging low, they could have been the only two people in Stilton.

"I have to say it," Holly blurted. "It's not like I've been waiting for you for fifteen years. I'm sorry, but I never thought of you as a boyfriend."

"Don't take this the wrong way, Holly, but other than pre-hormonal speculation, I didn't think of you that way either."

"Good." She squeezed his hand, joined with hers on the seat. "Good."

"I'm not sure I want you to be glad we were so obtuse."

"We were young."

He slowed as he approached the Kennedys' house. "Lights are on in the kitchen."

"Doug? Just Doug, do you think?"

"I doubt Bree slept. You know her better. Would she stay in her room or talk to her parents?"

Holly took a deep breath. "Let's find out."

He met her around her side of the truck. "You're supposed to wait for your boyfriend to assist you."

She snorted. "Like that's going to happen. I'm not too much different from what I was at twelve."

His gaze swept over her body. "You're right."

"Funny."

He proceeded up the frost-covered sidewalk and toward the back of the house. "If you won't hold my hand for your own safety, how about you make sure I don't fall instead?"

"I always suspected that was the motivation behind chivalry."

He dropped her hand as they neared the kitchen door. "No use flaunting our happiness."

"No." But she missed his hand around hers, even though she'd only experienced it for the past ten minutes of her life.

"Ready?" he asked.

Her nod signaled him to tap.

The curtain on the kitchen window twitched. Holly couldn't see who held it before it dropped. Latches turned and the door opened.

Holly's eyes widened. "Alan?"

CHAPTER NINE

Luke stepped in front of Holly, although he doubted Alan would become physical. Perhaps he and Bree had patched things up. "What's going on?"

Alan smirked then backed up to let them enter. "Bree and I are spending our wedding morning together."

"Wedding morning?" Holly asked.

"You're here early," Doug said from the table. An assortment of donuts and pastry boxes sat beside a fruit basket. "Look what Alan brought."

Bree walked into the room, pale and looking like she'd been crying. "I called him last night when I couldn't sleep."

Holly's gaze went to Doug and back to Bree. "And?"

Bree stood taller and put her arm through the crook of Alan's elbow. "We're getting married."

"Of course you are." Doug glanced at their serious faces and frowned. "Was there any doubt?"

"Not for me," Alan declared.

Her father stood. "What's going on?"

They all waited for Bree's answer.

"Alan and I had some things to work out, Dad, but we're fine now. He's going to be an amazing and dedicated husband."

"I am." Alan kissed her hand. "Dedicated to your happiness."

Doug scowled. "Did you do something I should know about?"

"No, Dad," Bree cut in. "This is between us." She turned to Holly. "Let's go in the living room."

Luke turned to Alan. "Help me bring in something from the car."

They stepped out different doorways, leaving Bree's dad wearing an unsettled frown.

"What do you need to get?" Alan hunched his shoulders. "It's like a freaking twenty degrees out here."

"Nothing." Luke stopped out of sight of the house. "What happened? How is the wedding still on?"

"Holly informed Bree she'd seen me on Monday. I explained to Bree how sleeping with LaTisha made me realize how much I loved her and wanted to marry her. Bree, that is, not LaTisha." He rubbed his arms. "She called me a few names, cried a little, then forgave me. But if I step out of line, she'll get out the meat cleaver." Alan grinned. "Quite the spitfire is my Bree."

Luke couldn't believe it. Not only had Alan gotten off the hook so easily, he didn't seem to appreciate that he'd almost lost Bree. The jerk stood before him, more concerned with the cold than his woman's heartbreak. "You don't deserve her."

"I've learned my lesson. I'm not going to cheat again. Although, as I've said before, we weren't even engaged last week, so it doesn't count."

If Doug heard him say that, he'd plant a fist in the idiot's face. Luke considered, with pleasure, doing the honors for Bree's dad. "No, it counted, jackass."

"Well, Bree got over it, so don't let it freak you out. Just drop it, okay? And if you have any influence over Holly, make sure she drops it, too."

"How have we stayed friends all these years?"

Alan shrugged. "We haven't seen much of each other since high school."

"That would be it. When I think of you, I think of that kid. Today, though, I can see that you're an idiot, only now you wear a nice suit."

Alan's jaw clenched. "The wedding's this afternoon. Do you want to be my best man or not?"

Luke pretended to consider, watching Alan sweat it out. The man's expression grew more mulish. Luke shook his head. "If Bree is foolish enough to marry you, I'll be there to make sure you show up."

"That's not a ringing endorsement. You're supposed to be my friend."

"It's the best I can do."

Holly crossed her arms around her ribs, holding in her nerves. And her breakfast. For the first time in their friendship, she couldn't read Bree's expression. This could go either way. Bree forgiving Alan gave her hope. If Bree could forgive infidelity, she could forgive honesty. It was a far less serious trespass. Or had she forgiven Alan *instead* of Holly?

Bree sat. Holly perched across from her in the same position she'd been in half a dozen hours before, telling her about Alan's betrayal. She swallowed hard, noting her friend's red-rimmed eyes and chapped nose.

"I'm sure you think I'm stupid for going through with the wedding."

"No, I don't, Bree. I want you to do whatever makes you happy."

"Alan makes me happy." Bree grimaced. "I'm not saying I'm thrilled with him right now, but he's really sorry. I believe him when he says it taught him how important I am to him."

Holly couldn't stomach the thought of Bree trusting Alan with her future, but it wasn't her decision. She nodded acceptance, hoping Bree wouldn't make her grovel. How broken was their friendship?

"I know what you're thinking."

Holly looked at her. "What am I thinking?"

"That I chose him over you."

Holly drew back. "No. Not even close. It wasn't a contest."

"Not a contest, but I had to take sides. If I marry Alan--when I marry Alan, will we still be friends? I can't have my best friend and my husband snarling at each other every time we're together."

"I... Okay, look." Holly took a breath. "I'm not as forgiving as you are, probably because I don't love him. It's your life and your husband-to-be, not mine. I can't promise to trust him, Bree. Your happiness is too important."

She figured her words disqualified her for maid of honor. How could Bree want her when Holly didn't like the groom? "I'm sorry if I ruined things, Bree. I didn't want you walking down the aisle not knowing what he did. You had to start your marriage off honestly."

Bree nodded. "I understand that, Holly. Do you think I don't know you at all? You didn't tell me to hurt me. You didn't even really tell me to break up the wedding plans."

Holly sagged with relief. "No, I didn't."

"Can you stand beside me while I marry Alan today?"

"Do you still want me to?" Holly couldn't believe it. Her chest expanded as though filled with helium.

"I do." Bree grinned. "I'm going to say those promises to

Alan with my eyes wide open. He's not perfect. Matter of fact, he just proved he can be a total ass. This was the first of the obstacles we'll have to navigate. Holly, I'm going to need you. You're the only one who knows us, who knows about this."

"Except Luke."

"I'm not worried about him telling anyone. Plus, Luke can punch out Alan if things get messy."

Holly laughed. "I think he has."

"Right, when we were in high school. I'd forgotten. So." Bree stood. "Will you be my maid of honor?"

"Yes." Holly rose and the two friends embraced.

"Thank you," Bree said into her ear. "I know how hard it was to tell me. I didn't make it easier."

"God, Bree, I didn't expect you could."

"I just froze inside." She hugged Holly to her, and they rocked side to side. "It hurt so much."

Holly blinked back tears. "I know. I'm sorry. I'm so sorry."

"I know you are."

"Would you have rather not known?" Holly sought confirmation she hadn't done more harm than good.

Bree pulled back and looked at her while considering. "I needed to know, and how could you *not* tell me?"

Holly chuckled and shook her head. "That's what I kept saying to Luke. Wait till I get him alone." A similar threat had her thinking of earlier with Luke. The image of a chocolate-drizzled banana had her coughing with embarrassment. "Uh, never mind."

Bree stared. "Oh. My. God. You and Beanpole Ivey?"

"No." Holly shifted, looked at the gift table, back at Bree. "Well, maybe. We don't know yet."

"That's the worst idea I've ever heard."

Holly gaped, astounded that Bree, her best friend--who was marrying a man who cheated on her two days before proposing marriage--could say that. "Why?"

"He lives in Stilton. He lives *for* Stilton, Holly. He's a local business owner. A volunteer fireman. This isn't just a place to him, it's his lifeblood." Bree rolled her eyes. "Besides, it's not like he can grow trees in Chicago."

"Don't say it like we don't have trees."

"Right, sorry. He could work for the park department for two dollars an hour raking leaves." Bree held up her hand in a halting motion. "I know you don't care about him making money, Holly, but he will."

Bree's lack of support hurt. Holly closed herself off. "We'll work it out."

"I hope so."

"So you don't see anything wrong with our being together, other than employment?"

"Luke's a great guy. He helps repair homes for seniors. He volunteers with the fire department. He has free or heavily discounted bonfires and hayrides for those who can't pay. In short, the guy's a freaking saint."

"But he's not good enough for me?"

"It's not a matter of him being good enough. You're too different. He's a country boy, Holl. He lives and breathes Stilton."

"I see."

"Now I've hurt your feelings." Bree touched her arm. "I don't mean to. This isn't payback or anything."

"I know. I didn't think that." Holly's disappointment ran deeper than hurt feelings. Because she feared Bree related the true picture. Luke would be miserable in the city. Maybe anywhere away from Stilton.

"Let's go find the guys and eat donuts," Bree said. "We're not going to solve this problem right now, and we have a lot to do."

Holly found a smile. "Because you're getting married in..." She glanced at the wall clock. "Just over six hours."

Bree squealed. "I am. I really am."

Luke and Alan ran Holly's car over to the Kennedys then raced with unseemly haste from the scene of the pre-wedding preparations. Luke hadn't had much of a chance to see Holly but gathered the women's friendship held firm. Still, something bothered Holly. He could see it in the frown around her eyes when she thought no one watched her.

But his new hobby was watching Holly MacDonald. Which sounded creepy. He cleaned up his house and changed his sheets. Maybe it was too soon to make love to Holly, despite their parking lot discussion. But he could plan ahead, just in case. And he couldn't help but think about it.

Kissing the girl that taught him to gig frogs had turned out pretty spectacular. He couldn't wait to see what else he could learn from her. He had plans for what he would share with her.

They'd have to figure out the logistics because this relationship mattered. He already needed Holly back in his life permanently, so things would have to work out. For him, it was a done deal, and he'd seen enough affection from Holly to hope she felt the same. They had to get through the wedding, then they would spend the next few days enjoying their first Christmas together. He'd solve this problem of where they'd live and how they'd spend together while being with the woman he'd fallen for so completely. She'd left him before. This time, he wasn't letting her live somewhere without him.

He picked up the groom and arrived at the church early, as nervous about seeing Holly again as he was about riding herd on Alan. He served as the only usher, worrying about Alan slipping out the back as he rolled out the paper carpet cover and seated the major family members. He wouldn't put anything past the moron.

With all the guests seated, he followed Alan out to the altar. His new dark gray suit looked sharp beside Alan's black. He hoped it pleased Holly, as she'd see it for the next few years.

The music changed. Luke shifted to catch a glimpse of Holly. He waited while Bree's cousin trembled her way down the aisle. Then Holly appeared at the door and his breath caught.

She wasn't the most beautiful woman he'd ever seen. She wasn't wearing the most provocative dress. She was just Holly.

Her gaze connected with his and they both smiled as she came toward him. The hairs on his neck rose. It felt almost as if he waited at the altar for her. Before he realized it, he'd gone down to the third or fourth pew to escort her the rest of the way. Her eyes lit with surprise and, he hoped, pleasure. Fortunately, not many people knew this hadn't been the plan all along.

They separated with a lingering touch and he returned to his spot to wait for Bree. Alan leaned over to him as the first chords of the traditional bridal march played. "Are you nuts? She's totally wrong for you."

Luke's face hardened. "Your bride is coming."

Alan jerked around just as Bree and Doug stepped onto the white paper runner.

The ceremony went off as usual. Luke stayed on edge, not rejoicing as he should have as his friend began a new stage of his life. A supposedly happier stage. Although relieved Bree had forgiven Alan, Luke just couldn't wring any enjoyment out of the ceremony. The marriage seemed doomed.

Alan's voice stayed strong as he promised to remain faithful. Luke caught Holly's eye when Bree emphasized, "till *death* do we part." Hopefully, Alan wouldn't cause her to use that meat cleaver she'd threatened him with, but Luke had little doubt Bree would wield it with pleasure if he broke his vow. Throughout the ceremony, Bree radiated joy, and that helped reconcile him to the possibility for their happiness.

Luke prayed for their harmonious life together.

He stole glances at Holly throughout the ceremony as they each performed their duties. She wiped at a tear now and again. He hoped they were tears of sentiment, not sorrow over Bree's future. The pink jacket made Holly's creamy skin even more incandescent. She smiled just for him. He added a quick prayer for his and Holly's happiness.

They signed the marriage certificate, posed for pictures and helped serve cake and punch in the church basement. He hated to admit he couldn't wait to get the day over and done.

After Alan and Bree had their first dance, Luke pulled Holly into his arms amid applause from the guests. Marie's boyfriend escorted her onto the dance floor. "Finally," Luke said into Holly's hair. "I have you to myself."

"With eighty people watching."

"I'll take what I can get."

"Well, they did it. They got married, with only five days between proposal and ceremony."

"Did you know Illinois had such a lax waiting period?" Luke asked.

"I had no idea. One day is insane. People can get married on an impulse."

"It does require twenty-four hours."

She laughed. "That's just a long impulse."

He twirled her and drew her in close again. "You don't believe in acting rashly?"

"I don't believe in marrying rashly." She waggled her eyebrows at him. "What else did you have in mind?"

"As soon as the happy couple departs, I suggest we head to my house."

"I can't."

"Oh. Well, all right. Sure. I understand." They danced for a few seconds while he considered the hitch in his plan. Had something changed her mind about them romancing each other? "Why not? I'm not suggesting we have sex or anything. Not yet."

"Really? That's a relief."

He narrowed his eyes at her. "Very funny. Why can't you come over?"

"I didn't say that. I said I couldn't head to your place from here." She smiled at him. "I thought I might check out of the motel. Take advantage of...your guest room."

He laughed with relief. "Honey, you can take advantage of whatever you want."

They toasted the couple's happiness with sincere wishes. Bree tossed the bouquet, and as arranged, Marie caught it. Luke and Holly escorted the bride and groom to Alan's car, and Holly fussed over stuffing Bree's train inside securely. Everyone waved and threw bird seed.

"I hope they'll be happy," Holly said.

"Of course they will," Anne Kennedy remarked. "If ever two people were meant to be together, it's them."

Luke exchanged glances with Doug over the ladies' heads. "I'm sure they will be," Luke said, wishing he felt more sure.

Doug glowered. "They'd better be."

The people in earshot laughed.

Once back in the church basement, Luke made sure Doug and Anne were set, said his goodbyes to Tony and the ever-unnerving Jim Henry and Lorraine, and dragged Holly out the door.

"Alone at last." He turned to her in her car and kissed her. "I've been waiting all day to do that."

"Me, too."

"Really?"

She nodded. "But I'm also planning to stay in the guest bedroom."

"I wouldn't have it any other way."

They laughed.

And spent the night laughing. Released from the drama of Bree and Alan's wedding, they cuddled up in their pajamas on the couch and watched *It's a Wonderful Life* followed by *Miracle on 34th Street*. When the bird clock in the kitchen screeched the midnight hour, Holly turned to Luke. "I've got to get some sleep."

"I thought you'd never say that." He grinned. "I didn't want to be the first to call it a night, and I want to spend every minute with you I can, but I'm almost dead."

She giggled. "Here I was thinking, 'jeez, just go to bed already.'"

"We're quite the romantic couple."

"Luke." She put her palm on his cheek. "I had more fun watching movies with you than I've had in a long while."

"I'll settle for fun since I'm too tired for romance."

She rose. "What are your plans for tomorrow? I promised Anne I'd help her box up the wedding gifts so she can reclaim her house for Christmas. I'm taking the fragile items back north with me Tuesday."

"You're leaving Christmas Day?"

"I have to be at work on Wednesday."

"So we only have tomorrow together."

She shook her head at him. "And Christmas. I won't have

to leave until four. I have to drop off the gifts at my house then return the car to my friend."

"Can you swing by your friend's house first and have her take you to your place? Then you'd have help carrying stuff in."

"I can't ask her to come out on Christmas."

Luke went still. "You mean, except for driving you home, right?"

"It's a nice neighborhood and the train is close."

"You can't take the train after dark. How far is the walk from the El stop to your apartment?"

"Not far."

"Holly, be sensible. You can't walk around Chicago like that."

"You've never been to my part of town. How do you know it's not safe?" She tried not to be exasperated, but he regarded all of her town as a criminal haven.

"Nowhere is safe for a woman alone."

"Hold on." She set her hands on her hips and took a minute to gather her patience. "First, there are areas that are safer than others, I'll give you that. I live in a mostly safe area. Second, I can defend myself, and if that fails, I can run fast. Third, I'm not stupid. I've been living in different big cities for several years. These past four, I've lived in different parts of Chicago."

"I don't mean to imply you're not capable."

"Good. I appreciate your concern."

"But you're going to ignore me."

"I'm going to ask you to trust me to be careful. Now, let's talk about something more pleasant. What time is church?"

He scowled at her change of subject. "At five and eleven. The five o'clock is full of kids, but the music is more upbeat. The eleven o'clock service is more solemn as Christmas Day arrives, but the choir does most of the singing. It's a nice performance."

"Pros and cons to each option. I like the way you think."

"Do you have a preference?"

"I want the upbeat music and the kids. But I also want to soak in the solemnity of the holiday."

Luke groaned. "Don't tell me you want to go to both services."

"You can choose which to go to with me."

"We'll go to both together. But next year, you have to choose one."

She got a thrill to hear him speak of them together next year. "We'll see. I'll grab my own breakfast before I go help Anne. Don't feel you have to stick around if you need to get to work because I'm probably going to sleep late."

"Micah has the morning shift, and I got up about the same time you did this morning. I might sleep in, too."

"Then maybe I'll see you in the morning." She smiled, feeling her way through the sudden awkward tension.

"You go on up," Luke said. "I'll lock up down here."

"Oh, okay. Goodnight."

"Holly."

She turned at the stairs.

"If I kiss you, I won't want to stop, and it's too early in our relationship and too late at night for that."

His explanation eased her worry. "Thanks for telling me."

It's like he can read my mind still. She put her hand on the railing and climbed the stairs. Their connection drew her in. His thoughtfulness made it easy to love him.

She missed a step and bumped her toe. *Love him? Already?*

But he had nothing nice to say about the city and feared for her safety there. What if their relationship worked out and their futures merged? She couldn't leave Chicago and he couldn't leave here.

This was so not good.

CHAPTER TEN

Holly jumped out of bed, excited to start the day with Luke. The clock on the nightstand indicated she'd slept until eight. She stretched and yawned, then bounced into the bathroom. A brisk shampooing rinsed away the last of the hairspray from the wedding 'do. She emerged herself once again.

Jeans and a sweater over a T-shirt warmed her and looked good enough for whatever they wound up doing. They'd already been to a nice restaurant, if the tense rehearsal dinner counted, so something simple fit her level of energy for the day. She needed to find time to shop and think of a present for Luke. Unfortunately, Bree was her go-to-girl for shopping.

She wandered down the stairs, alert for signs of his presence. Coffee perfumed the air, compelling her like the most potent aphrodisiac.

Disappointed to find the kitchen empty, she almost set the milk on top of his note.

Sorry I missed you this morning.

> Gone to work. The place sounds crazy.
> Which is good. Be home around two if I can or three at the latest.
> I'm sorry we can't spend more time together.
> *Luke*

She liked the sound of "be home around two." Not the part where he'd be late, but the normal, everyday expectation. Maybe this is what Doug and Anne expressed at the rehearsal dinner with his easy acceptance of her drinking and the kiss on her forehead. As she'd told Bree, not everything had to do with sex.

The house key sitting beside the note made her smile. Cautious Luke giving out a key three days into the relationship had to be a record.

Holly gulped down some toast and coffee then drove over to help Anne. They reboxed what they could for safe transport and wrapped the rest of the fragile items in newspaper. "Can I ask you something?" Holly said.

"Of course."

"Do you have any spare ideas for a gift for a man? For Luke?"

Anne grinned. "Are you two a couple? I knew it!"

"We're trying it on." Great. Their relationship was a sweater. "Trying it out," she corrected, making them a new car. "We're trying."

"That's wonderful. You two are the second cutest couple your age."

"So I've heard."

Anne tapped her finger against her lip. "Now, you need a present."

"He's pretty special and this is our first holiday together. I've known him for my entire life, but I've also only known him for a few days."

"Now I'm worried."

"Why?"

"Because I understood that." Anne laughed.

"There must be something in the Stilton water. The town is full of comedians."

"Sorry. Will you forgive me if I feed you lunch?"

"Absolutely."

Anne led the way into the kitchen. She pulled open the refrigerator and stared at the contents. "My suggestion is to wander past the shops on Main Street. If you're supposed to buy something for Luke, you'll know."

Goosebumps rose on Holly's arms. "Like, it'll call to me?"

"I didn't say that. Exactly. Ham or turkey sandwich?"

So, an hour later, Holly had loaded her car with wedding presents, drove to the downtown area, and easily found a place to park. She wandered the street, feeling both discouraged and silly as she passed each shop and nothing magical happened.

She'd lost her mind.

None of the storefronts looked like Luke, either. She paused for a moment in front of a fabric store. The woman inside looked familiar. When she turned and waved, exposing her swollen belly, Holly remembered her from Santa's Cabin. Her adorable son, Tyler, had thanked Santa for his new dad. Holly waved back, feeling a connection. She actually knew someone in town she hadn't gone to school with.

She couldn't resist the yarn shop next door and came out with locally raised and spun wool for her sister's birthday in February. A store called the Greenery turned out to be recycled and organic items. She purchased recycled crayons molded into trucks for her nephews. She'd already sent their Christmas presents, but a January boredom-killer wouldn't go amiss. Nothing seemed right for Luke.

Resolutely, she crossed the street to walk back to her car. She ordered carryout from the Dew Drop In and enjoyed a pop while waiting. Holly hummed along to the overhead Christmas music as she watched people pass by the windows. It seemed every person called out to someone or was hailed. What would it be like to live so closely interwoven with twenty thousand other people?

She gathered the food bag and headed out. Three stores down, she heard her name. And Luke's. Someone exited and she realized her name had come from inside a store. Music.

"The Holly and the Ivy" played over the store's speakers. She'd heard "Holly...Ivey" and halted in her tracks. Now she stepped inside and looked around. A bookstore.

"Welcome to Buy the Book," a woman called from near a shelf where she restocked books. "All our books are ten percent off today. I'm Claire. If I can help you find a title, please let me know."

Holly couldn't speak, she was so amazed. Anne had said to walk down the street and if she was supposed to buy something for Luke, she'd know it when she passed the right store. This place had called her name--both their names. She was used to hearing "holly" mentioned at Christmastime, but this experience left her heart thudding.

Had the half dozen or so other shoppers been lured into the store?

She glided over to the counter as if pulled by a stronger force. "I bet you keep wish lists."

The woman looked at her, sweeping her strawberry blond hair behind an ear. "That's a great idea, but no, we don't. We will next year, though."

Holly frowned as the woman came to the counter and scribbled a note. "I don't understand. I thought there'd be something..."

"Yes?"

She felt as bewildered as Natalie Wood's character

searching under the tree for a note about her present from Kris Kringle. "I thought there would be a present here for me to buy."

Claire smiled. "If you're looking for a book, then yes, this is the place. What does the person to whom you're giving it like to read?"

Holly thought back to Luke's bookshelves. "Everything."

"Oh, that makes it easier and harder, doesn't it? Maybe the classics? Or you might purchase something just released."

Holly perked up. "There's an idea. Do you keep anything new on hold for customers? Maybe where you've called but he hasn't picked it up?"

Claire waved a hand at a bookcase behind the counter. "That's what those are."

"Excellent," Holly said. "Do you have anything in for Luke Ivey?"

The clerk nodded. "Oh, sure, Luke's a regular here. If there's something waiting, do you want to buy it for him or just see that you don't duplicate it?"

"Buying it will make my holiday so much easier." She added an older book about traversing the Appalachian Trail for Micah. She picked out a sewing mystery for Anne and a runner's diary for Doug. Claire wrapped the purchases at no extra charge.

Maybe this place really was magic.

Holly rushed back to Luke's and put their dinner in the fridge and the gifts under the three foot tall tree on a side table in a corner. If it hadn't been for the smell of pine, she wouldn't have known he had a tree. He hadn't turned on the lights any time she'd been there.

She pulled out her phone to call him then reconsidered. Was it too early in their relationship to call him at work? Would he think she was nagging or needing to be entertained?

Instead she skimmed his shelves to better gauge his taste in fiction for presents later on. As she recalled her experience at the store, she started to laugh. "Oh. Good. Grief."

If she married Luke, her name would be Holly Ann Ivey.

Maybe she hadn't heard two names being called. Maybe she'd heard her future name. A chill ran over her. Premonition?

If Fate meant her to marry the man, she could interrupt his work. She threw a couple of oranges and bottles of water in a canvas bag. After adding another layer of clothes, she hopped in the car.

Five minutes later, she discovered the Orchard parking lot half-full. Why the crowd? She'd figured people would be home wrapping presents and dressing for church. If they had presents left to buy, they should be on Main Street and the other downtown shops. What did the Ivey Orchard carry that would bring in so many people on Christmas Eve afternoon?

Five people stood around the hot chocolate stand while

others browsed through wreaths, garland and cemetery blankets. She didn't spot Luke in the crowd but spied Micah with a customer. When he led the woman to the counter to check out with a college-aged boy, she hailed him. "What's going on here?"

Surprising her, Micah leaned in and kissed her cheek. "Other than my brother humming Christmas tunes and smiling like a moron all morning?"

"What makes you think I have anything to do with that?" But a grin stretched her cold cheeks, as well.

"Thank you, Holly, seriously. Our mom died between Thanksgiving and Christmas. Luke carries that with him every year. Luckily, we're usually too busy during that time for him to dwell on losing her."

Micah turned to answer a question from a customer. She thought of Luke's unlit tree, shoved in a corner. "Thanks for telling me," she said when Micah finished. "Do you cut the greenery here for the garland?"

"Of course."

"Do you custom design the wreaths or ship out the work?"

Micah shifted on his feet, looking at the floor. "I made them."

She eyed him with surprise. "Really?"

"I used to date a florist. She showed me how."

"Well, aren't you the information gatherer?" she teased.

He leered. "That's not all she taught me."

"Please." Holly held up a hand, laughing. "No details."

"What's with the questions?"

"I was thinking you could offer custom-made, while-you-wait wreaths. Get in some ribbons, pine cones and whatnot. Maybe hit the after-Christmas sales for plastic doves or cardinals." She shrugged. "It might draw people."

"Not a bad idea." He stared into a corner as though envisioning the setup. "I could teach someone to do the wreaths, but I usually have the bows made by someone else."

"There are bow-tying videos online. Someone could learn."

"I'm liking this idea."

Enthused, Holly went on. "You could have a demonstration here one night early in December. It would bring in people. They could buy supplies from you and make their own."

"Possibly. We'd need tables and chairs, wire cutters."

"If you led it, all the women in town would come." She grinned. "Just think, all your old girlfriends in one room."

He laughed. "Yeah, forget it. That's so not going to happen."

"Okay, then. How about a guys' night? Show the men how easy and less expensive making a wreath can be."

"Men? Men from around here?" He shook his head. "No

one would show."

"You're their guru, Micah. Everyone knows the women flock after you. If you can build a wreath, any farmer around here can. You'll make holiday decorating a manly activity." She grinned. "Bring in some TVs and peanuts and watch football while you all work."

"Holly, you're a genius."

"And you should start charging for that hot chocolate. Fifty cents a cup or something minimal to cover your costs."

"Holly, you *were* such a genius."

Surprised, she stepped back. "What?"

Micah shook his head. "Luke will never go for it. I'm not sure *I* would go for it. Free hot chocolate is an Ivey tradition."

"I'm trying to keep you from going broke. Keep the idea in mind."

He directed a woman to an aisle with bird feeders. "Thanks for the other suggestions, though. I'm seeing opportunities to--pardon the pun--grow the business."

She laughed. "What are your plans for tonight and tomorrow? Is there a brother thing you guys do? I don't want to get in the way."

He appeared as though he wanted to speak but hesitated.

"If you guys have plans, I'm fine on my own. God knows, there are books to read. But if it's not awkward, I'd like to be included."

Micah's forehead furrowed. "I don't know if you'd consider it awkward. How *do* you feel about strip joints?"

Her mouth dropped open in shock before he started laughing. After an instant of feeling foolish, she joined in. "One of these days, Micah Ivey. One of these days."

"Sorry," he said, although clearly not, as he continued to chuckle. "We have a meal and exchange presents. There's no set tradition. Might be dinner either night or lunch. It depends on whether Luke is dating anyone seriously and what her plans are."

"Do you ever date anyone seriously?"

"Ah, jeez." He rolled his eyes. "You go to a wedding and fall for my brother, and now you're trying to tie me down?"

"Sorry. I've always felt like your big sister, but I'll back off." She patted his arm. "So, what was the plan this year? Dinner tonight?"

She could stretch the Dew Drop turkey dinners to feed a third person. She'd make some more mashed potatoes and another vegetable dish. Imagining glazed carrots in butter and brown sugar made her mouth water.

All of a sudden, she'd become part of a family, not just a couple, if only for these two days. "I'd like you to come over if you don't have a date."

"I don't know. Luke told me our plans were on hold. I don't want to step on his game."

She giggled. "That man has no game. He's incredibly straight-forward, which makes him unbelievably appealing." She thought of him setting her straight in the parking lot. Luke didn't play games, and Holly's anticipation sharpened while she waited for him to reveal his assertiveness. Maybe his making her wait was a game? She turned back to Micah. "I'm inviting you."

He raised a hand in farewell to a customer. "Then I'm coming."

"Alone?"

"I prefer to fly solo at Christmas, but this year, I am dating someone. I don't know why we haven't broken up yet." His mouth twisted as though mocking himself. "But she's gotten sicker, so yeah, it'll just be me."

She shook her head. If she and Luke figured out how to be together, Micah was her next project. "Okay, dinner at six, church at eleven?"

"Sounds good. I'll bring apple cider we make here in the Fall, and I have a cherry pie from the bakery."

She leaned down to inspect his averted face. "Are you blushing?"

He shifted his weight. "The woman at the bakery is new in town. She wrote her phone number--and address--inside the lid of the box."

"I'm sure that's par for the course for you. Why the red

cheeks?"

"I'm still dating Jayne, the school teacher," he reminded her. "It feels underhanded to get someone else's number while we're together, and especially because she's sick. It's not like I went out looking for a replacement."

His viewpoint contrasted glaringly with Alan's. She hugged him. "Don't worry about it, Micah. I'm sure Jayne understands you can't be accountable for other women lusting after you."

He laughed. "I'll tell her you said so."

"Okay, I've been here ten minutes, and while I've enjoyed talking to you, I haven't caught sight of your brother. Where's Luke?"

"He'd just left for the balsam orchard to cut down a tree when you arrived."

Lumberjack Luke? Oh, this she had to see.

Micah gave her directions and she yanked on the red hat. It was a good five minute hike past the fruit trees before she began winding through evergreens that looked pretty much the same to her. Fortunately, she followed the buzz of a chain saw before it stopped. She rounded a row in time to see Luke lop off the bottom of a tree positioned across a wagon bed. A green tractor hitched in front to pull the wagon. Must be the hay ride wagon, she thought, noting its benches across each side.

"That look like the right height?" Luke asked the family

around him.

"Don't cut off any more," a girl of about six cried.

"It looks fine," the father declared.

The girl and her three brothers whooped and jumped around.

Luke lifted and reset the tree more securely on the wagon bed. She hated to be such a cliché, but seeing him do something so physical made her blood race. *You man, me woman. Come closer.*

As though hearing her thoughts, Luke looked up at her and smiled before whipping off his protective glasses. He'd donned a gray stocking cap, but his cheeks were red from the below freezing temperature.

"Hey, Holly." He turned to the family. "Excuse me for a minute. Why don't you all climb on board."

He came to her, obeying her silent directive. He smelled of the outdoors, pine sap, and cut wood, and he carried the saw. "I shouldn't kiss you with little eyes watching."

"It's fine. You can owe me one."

He laughed. "I have to take them back to the store, but I can have Sean wrap the tree and help load it in their car. They paid in October, so it'll just take a minute to hand them off."

He looked frozen through, so she abandoned the idea of eating oranges under the sun. She raised her voice so it would carry to the wagon. "Can you show me this tree in the next row?

I might want it for my place."

The mom raised a hand in acknowledgement while the dad grinned.

"I see you're wearing your new hat," Luke said.

"My boyfriend bought it for me."

Once on the other side of the tree line, Holly grabbed Luke's jacket and pulled him in for a kiss. They warmed each other as one kiss turned into a second and third. "Do you have time for a break in your office or lunch room?"

His eyes went wide. "In the lunch room?"

She thumped his chest with the back of her hand. "I brought oranges."

"Kinky."

This Ivey family had a bizarre sense of humor, she thought. But she still wore her smile as she climbed onto the wagon seat.

"These are the Gibsons," Luke said. "This is Holly."

"Are you Mr. Ivey's girlfriend?" the little girl asked.

"I guess I am."

"She is," Luke countered more firmly before heading to the front.

The girl and her brothers giggled. Their mother shushed them as Luke started up the tractor.

He handed them off as promised to the gangly boy who'd been behind the counter. "Micah sent me out," the boy said with a grin.

Holly hustled inside out of the cold while Luke gave instructions and said his goodbyes and thank yous to the Gibsons.

He came in and took her elbow. "I have an office in the back."

Bookshelves and file cabinets filled the space not taken up by a dented gray metal desk. She itched to find a spray can of paint and refresh the color. Forest green or cranberry would suit him. Or navy with cranberry legs to add a bit of adventure while remaining business-like.

"I have no idea what you're thinking," Luke said.

"You might find out. Is your office ventilated?"

He blinked. "Beg your pardon?"

"I'm not talking about sex." She set the tote bag on his desk. "This place will smell like oranges for a week."

"It'll remind me of you."

"Does Micah share this office?" Holly pulled out a pocket knife from her purse. She raised her eyebrows, questioning Luke's grin. "What? You didn't think I'd carry a knife with me?"

"I figured you'd have a switchblade. For protection."

His reminders of the dangers of the big city began to irk her. She shrugged it off. Once he visited and experienced the wonders of Chicago, he'd come to appreciate the city. She hoped.

They fed each other orange slices between kisses. She informed him of the change of plans for the evening.

He frowned. "I wanted to spend our first Christmas Eve alone with you."

"Micah is family, and his girlfriend is sick. I didn't want him to be alone."

"Okay. We have tomorrow. Thanks for making dinner."

"Well, the kind people at the Dew Drop In helped a little."

He smirked. "Is that a fact?"

"They're closing at five today, so I did them a favor by taking all that food off their hands."

"You're too good to them." He kissed her. "I didn't expect you to slave away all day, Holly. Micah and I had reservations."

"Where?"

When he grinned, she laughed. "Romero's? It's a little too soon for me to go there. Be sure to cancel your reservation so they can fill the table."

"Yes, ma'am."

"Hey, I waitressed for two years in college. Those people deserve our consideration." She rose and packed up the trash.

"I'll be heading home in half an hour. Why don't you stay?"

"Sorry. I've got some things to do still at your place before dinner."

"Don't go overboard. Micah and I are bachelors. Our bar is pretty low."

She kissed him. "I'll have to work on that."

"I'm not kidding. For Thanksgiving, Micah grilled turkey burgers."

"Wow. I'm feeling far less intimidated now."

Holly rushed through the grocery store with other shoppers before it closed then hurried to Luke's. The jar of jellied cranberry sauce went into the freezer for a quick chill. She put in her earbuds and brought up Christmas tunes on her player. Before long, potatoes boiled on the stove. She transferred the dinners onto serving dishes to warm in the oven and microwave.

Then she plugged in the Christmas tree lights and pulled the table away from the wall so the tree became part of the room rather than an inconvenient visitor. She lit bayberry candles and set out cinnamon sticks around the living room and in the kitchen.

As an afterthought, she ran upstairs and put a candle and cinnamon stick in Luke's bedroom. She changed into a candy-striped Oxford shirt and slacks. A quick hair brushing and a flash of lipstick brightened her outlook. It would have to do.

The front door opened. Excited, she ran down the stairs.

"Honey, I'm home." Luke grinned.

Her heart skipped with joy despite his joking. What would it be like for them to come home to each other every night? A handsome man who wanted to be with her. How had she gotten so lucky?

She'd seen reruns of old sitcoms and recognized Luke's line as the typical greeting from a 1950s TV husband. At least, she *hoped* he wasn't quoting the creepy scene from *The Shining*. How would an obedient, 1950s TV wife respond? "How was your day, dear?"

He swept her into his arms, her feet leaving the floor. "Long, but I had a nice break in the afternoon."

His kiss made her toes curl before he set her down. He removed his coat, then turned and pulled open the door. Micah stood on the porch.

"I heard you coming," Luke said.

"I didn't want to track snow in from the patio." Micah eyed Luke's retreating back as he went up the stairs and then kissed Holly's cheek. "I usually come in the kitchen, like the other morning. Thanks for inviting me."

"It's the Ivey family dinner. Thanks for letting me barge in."

Micah smiled. "I heard you barged in with food, so all is forgiven." He held out the bouquet of white roses, juggling the sack in his arms. "I brought that pie and cider, and these are for you."

"They're perfect, Micah. Thank you." She sniffed their heady scent and couldn't help teasing him. "That florist came in handy again."

"I snuck in just before closing. She was glad to get rid of these."

"Was she also glad to see you or did you break her heart?"

"She's married."

"Oooh, evading the question. Interesting." She laughed at his expression. Having a younger sibling was fun. "I just have to warm up the rolls."

Micah set the bag on the kitchen counter then strolled back to the tree. "It looks nice, Holly. Smells like Christmas, too."

They silently communicated understanding. She'd brought the holiday back to the Ivey brothers, and Micah appreciated it. He turned and set presents beneath the tree.

"What do you think about music?" Holly asked. "I have speakers and tons of Christmas tunes on my playlist."

Micah glanced at the ceiling. "I think we can risk it. Luke has a dock that should work."

They ate dinner amid much laughter and light conversation. Afterward the men cleaned the table and kitchen while Holly adjourned to the living room with coffee. She set aside worries about the future. For tonight, Luke being tied to the town and the business didn't bother her. Thoughts of what he'd find to do in Chicago for work would have to wait. She deserved a break. After the ordeal with Bree, she wanted to take two days to not fret about the next bad thing that might happen. She wanted them to open their presents, so she could enjoy the moment.

Luke sat down and put his arm around her. Micah took the chair opposite.

"Can you open your gifts now," she asked "or do you have to wait until Christmas morning?" She didn't want to disrupt their traditions. This relationship had advanced so fast, no one had had time to adjust. "These are from me, not Santa, so I think it would be okay."

The guys grinned at each other, then at her.

"You can't wait, can you?" Luke asked.

"No, I really can't."

Micah rose and handed Holly a package. "From me."

Her heart filled with love. "Thank you, Micah. I didn't expect anything."

"I'm not a total deadbeat." He said it jokingly, but she detected a layer of annoyance. She hadn't meant to hurt his feelings.

"I never thought you were a deadbeat. You guys have kept the Orchard going all these years. That takes hard work."

"Just open the present." But he smiled as he said it.

The paper tore back to reveal a jewelry box holding a silver "H" pendant on a chain. "It's beautiful. Thank you." She kissed him, before immediately fastening on the necklace. "I love it. Now open yours."

Luke grunted. "Hello, you two. I'm still here."

Holly laughed and grabbed the present she'd bought him. "Oh, for heaven's sakes. Here."

"You're too gracious." He kissed her. "This is what I really want."

"Gag me," Micah muttered.

"You should have asked Santa," Holly countered.

"I didn't want to wait until tomorrow. Fifteen years is long enough."

"Oh, my God," Micah groused as they kissed again.

Luke tore open the paper to uncover the mystery novel she'd bought him. "I've wanted to read this. How did you know?"

"Christmas magic. It kind of called my name."

The guys looked at her as she giggled.

"Yeah. Okay." Luke shrugged at Micah, who mouthed, "Humor her."

"Open yours," she said, handing a package to Micah.

He laid it on his lap and just looked at it. "You got me a book?"

"Yeah. Shouldn't I have?" When Micah continued to stare at the gift, she grew worried. Couldn't he read?

"No one ever gets me a book." His Ivey blue eyes shone when he glanced at Holly. "Cologne. Calendars. Food, wine. Luggage, even. But never a book."

Luke's arm went around her shoulders.

"So, is this a bad thing?" she asked into the silence.

"Thank you." Micah rose and kissed her cheek.

Relieved laughter escaped her. "You don't even know what it is."

"Doesn't matter. I already love it." But he removed the wrappings with care and eagerness. He flipped open the cover and scanned the flap. "It's about the AT? I've always talked about hiking the Appalachian Trail."

"You have?" She wouldn't have taken him for a hiker.

Micah grinned. "Are you trying to get rid of me?"

"Yes," Luke said.

"No," Holly said at the same time. She smacked Luke in the belly. "Of course I'm not."

"You be nice or I'll give your present to charity." Luke grabbed a package for her. "Merry Christmas, Holly. You've filled my life with warmth."

She opened a box to find the softest emerald green scarf she'd ever felt. "It's lovely. Cashmere?"

He nodded. "The yarn or whatever isn't local, but the crafter is. She sells her stuff at a shop on Main Street."

"The yarn store by the Greenery? I was in there today. That's a dangerous store for me."

"You can do that stuff?"

"I knit and crochet. Today I bought yarn to make a sweater for Daisy."

"Your sister? I haven't thought about her in years."

"Since you didn't think of me, you better not have thought of her. Or Poppy. Or Jack or Will or Amy, for that matter."

Micah laughed. "I never thought about it, but I guess there aren't any flowers named after boys."

"Sure there are. Like Sweet William and Jack in the pulpit."

Luke snorted. "Oh, man, seriously? I wish I'd know that when you guys lived here."

"Jack and Will both played football," Holly said of her brothers, "and you were a nerd. They'd have creamed you if you'd teased them."

"What are they doing now?" Micah asked.

"Will is a trust lawyer." She bit her lip to control her mirth. "Jack's a preacher."

The Ivey brothers fell off their seats laughing.

"Wait," Luke wheezed, "is Poppy a pharmacist?"

The question set Micah off again. Holly would confirm his guess later. At least Daisy and Amaryllis didn't have jobs connected to their names.

After they collected themselves, Luke and Micah handed each other presents. "It's cologne," Luke said, straight-faced.

"I got you a book."

"Guys," Holly admonished. "Stop it."

But she loved watching them together and being part of

their family. If things didn't work out, she'd always have this memory.

Luke unwrapped a black flannel shirt with a day planner tucked inside. "Thanks. I can write in dates with Holly."

Micah tore the paper from a box of cologne with gift cards taped to the back. "Perfect. At least you know what I wear and when I need more. These are great restaurants to take dates to. Thanks."

They cleaned up and watched "How the Grinch Stole Christmas." Then it was off to church. She stood in the pew between the Ivey brothers, reveling in their close bond and grateful both had accepted her into their lives again. She prayed no one would get hurt.

The choir had mastered several older hymns in Italian and Latin and featured a lovely young soprano. A violin and cello accompanied the organ. Holly was moved by the haunting guitar solo of "O, Holy Night."

Back out in the cold after the service, she huddled in the truck between Micah and Luke. She hadn't realized how much she missed her family until she'd found both a boyfriend and a brother. Micah acting as tagalong took her back to the days she'd lived next door to them.

Once back home, Micah stopped at his front door. "I'm sleeping in tomorrow. If you want some company, I might be dressed after eleven."

"Thanks for the warning." Luke and Micah exchanged that handshake and one-armed hug men did.

Holly kissed Micah's cheek. "Thanks for today. It was wonderful."

"You're welcome. Merry Christmas."

"Merry Christmas." She went in behind Luke.

"Well, now that we're rid of Little Brother," he said loudly.

"I heard that," Micah called back from the porch.

"You two."

The other door slammed, making Luke laugh. He grabbed her in a hug. "It was a good day, wasn't it?"

She nodded and laid her cheek against his heart. "Never had one better."

They swayed there, just inside the door, still wearing their coats.

After a long minute, Luke said, "Thanks for decorating, and putting the meal together, and making time to buy us both presents. It felt like Christmas should."

"I'm glad. Last week, I planned to spend Christmas reading a book I bought for myself for Christmas."

"We can snuggle up tomorrow and read all day."

"Luke, the point is, despite the presents from my family, I would have been alone again. You guys making me a part of your Christmas is the best present I could have received."

"How about my heart?"

"What?"

"I love you, Holly. It's too soon, and I'll probably damn myself for saying it before you're ready, but that's how I feel."

"It *is* too soon, but I've fallen in love with you, too, Lucas Ivey."

Several breathless minutes later, they found themselves on the couch, clothes rearranged and hair messy. "It's Christmas Day," Holly said.

"I think we missed Santa while we were at church."

"That's okay," she said. "He brought my gift early."

"We'll have to thank Alan for being a cheating scumball and getting us together again."

"The wedding would have brought us together. There was no need for him to be...himself." She frowned, worried for Bree.

"Stop." Luke smoothed back her hair. "It's done. She chose him. For better or for worse."

"I guess."

"And you gave her that choice to make, Holly. I think I was wrong about not telling Bree."

Holly raised her eyebrows in surprise. "Really? You felt so strongly about my interference."

"Maybe Alan will be a better husband knowing she could have walked away. That she had reason to walk, but she loved him enough to stand by him. Taking him on was a conscious decision on her part. Now he doesn't have to live with the secret between them."

"I didn't do it for him." So, Holly thought. Infidelity wasn't a gray area for Luke. He just abhorred the gossiping. That eased her mind.

Luke stood and pulled her to her feet. "I'm going to let you sleep in like Micah. Meet me in the kitchen around nine or so. I'll make omelets."

"I'm staying in the guest room tonight?" She couldn't decide if relief or disappointment dominated her emotions.

"I'm an idiot," Luke said, shaking his head, "but yes. Five days ago, we barely remembered each other's existence. I don't want to rush you into anything else."

Because things might not work out for them. She hadn't realized Luke harbored doubts, too. He always seemed so positive.

Would it be harder or easier to end their romance if they made love? Holly didn't know. Her respect for Luke rose. He could have suggested otherwise and they'd be naked already.

Love wasn't the problem. Just distance and lifestyles.

"I'm going on up then." She had a feeling she was about to experience a long winter's night--nap optional.

December 25th

Christmas Day passed too quickly. They did wind up

snuggling together on the couch and reading. Micah came, fully dressed, at eleven, then quickly went home and got his book. After an hour, Luke fried chicken for lunch, and they ate the leftover sides from dinner. She spent a quiet afternoon, reading with her two guys.

At three o'clock, Holly started watching the minute hand speed around the circle of the clock face. At half past three, she stretched and faced the facts. "It's time for me to go."

Micah jumped up and snatched her close. "I'll get out of you guys' hair. It was so good to see you again, Holly. Welcome back to Stilton. Welcome home."

She returned his hug. "I'm glad to be here."

"See you soon?"

Holly didn't know what to say. They hadn't made any plans. "I hope so."

With a scowl for Luke, Micah headed out.

"I hope you're coming back soon," Luke said. "But I was thinking I might come to you for New Year's."

A grin broke out in her heart and on her face. "I'd love that."

"Great. I can get away Friday night. We're closed on New Year's Eve and Day, so I could stay through the afternoon of the first, if that's all right."

"All right?" she enthused. "I get you for...four and half days? I'll take it."

"But I'll call you tonight."

"I'm so relieved. I didn't know when we'd see each other. When either of us could make time."

Luke grinned. "I'll bring my new day planner. We'll get our schedules straight and make this happen."

She threw her things back into her suitcase and pulled on her red cap. Neither of them wanted to break out of their embrace by the front door, but finally Luke pulled back. "I don't want you driving too late so you'd better get going. I'll worry, so call me once you've returned the car and are back home."

"I will." Tears pricked her eyes. She rushed out into the cold.

The days apart dragged by. On the day after Christmas, Holly completed the project that had been giving her difficulties only the week before. Her boss's praise pleased her but came at an inconvenient time. *Great. Now he appreciates my work?* Being overlooked again would have given her an excuse to leave her job and move to Stilton. Instead, she'd stepped further up the promotion ladder toward vice president of the marketing department.

"This merits a bonus," her boss said. "Our client will be pleased."

She smiled while thinking, *dammit*.

Luke called every night. He planned to visit for New Year's Eve, so she cleaned her apartment as though the Pope was coming. It distracted her, but she still spent too many lonely hours missing Luke. She cooked and froze meals so they could just pull out whatever appealed to them at that moment. She only had four days to show him Chicago's merits. Cooking wouldn't tie up her time or keep her anchored to the kitchen.

Then on Thursday night, Luke called with bad news. "I can't come tomorrow. I have to cover the store all weekend. I won't be there until the thirtieth, late. But I'm still coming, Holly."

Holly sank onto her couch, pressed down by disappointment. "What's wrong?"

"Micah. He's okay," Luke rushed to assure her. "But he fell off a ladder taking down decorations at our house."

"Oh, no."

"The idiot sprained his ankle and cracked a rib."

"Oh, my gosh. Poor Micah. How can I help?"

Luke sighed. "We're handling it, thanks. He can't use crutches because of the rib. He's bunking out on my sofa bed, bored and cranky."

"Who takes care of him while you're at work?"

"His girlfriend has been coming over, but she and her sister are going home to St. Louis to celebrate Christmas this weekend since they were sick for the actual day. School starts next Thursday, so I'll have to figure something out."

"I'm sorry, Luke. I can hear how tired you are."

"It's more that I'm disappointed for cancelling our plans. But Jayne's going to come back and stay over so you and I can spend New Year's Eve together. The Orchard will be closed. I'm sorry it can't be a longer visit."

"Me, too."

They talked for a few more minutes, but the air had leaked out of their joy balloon. Holly glanced around her immaculate living room, holding her cell phone to her chest. Not that cleaning was ever a wasted effort, but she'd done it for Luke. Now all her preparations seemed pointless.

Or were they?

CHAPTER ELEVEN

December 28th

Friday night, Holly tapped Luke's door with her boot since sacks loaded down her arms. He swung open the door and his mouth dropped open as well.

"Holly!" He grabbed two bags from her, planting a kiss on her temple, all he could reach. "What are you doing here?"

"Let her in," Micah called from behind him.

"Right, right." Luke stepped backward. "I'm just surprised to see you. I thought I heard a car, but I never imagined it would be you."

"How are you feeling, Micah?" she asked as Luke put the bags on the table.

"Better for seeing you. Are you staying all weekend?"

She handed her remaining bags off to Luke. "I am. If I'm welcome."

"Oh, baby." Luke leaned down and kissed her. "You are so welcome."

"If I say you're welcome," Micah asked, "do I get a kiss?"

"Absolutely." She leaned over the back of the sofa and kissed his head.

"Not the same," he complained.

"Not your girl," Luke countered.

"I've missed you boys."

Luke took her arm. "Come in the kitchen so we don't corrupt the kid."

She laughed and trailed along in his wake.

"Wait," Micah called as they passed behind him. "There's nothing good on TV. You can stay in here." After a moment, he called out, "I can hear you kissing back there."

When they still didn't emerge, he groaned.

Holly came around beside him several minutes later, patting down her hair. She sat on the coffee table and took Micah's hand. "Luke went out the mud room. He's bringing in the rest of my stuff, so we just have a second. How are you, really?"

"Bored. Frustrated. Angry at myself."

"In pain?"

"Some. It comes and goes." He growled under his breath. "I deserve it, though, that's what you're thinking. It was stupid of me not to double-check the ladder's footing."

She wasn't about to pity him, despite the lines around his mouth indicating it might be time for another pain pill. He needed a swift kick, not coddling. "Yeah, it was."

Micah blinked. "What?"

"You're not ten any more, Micah."

"I know." He had the grace to look shame-faced.

"If it helps any, I blame Luke for letting you get away with being charming and irresponsible for so long."

"Yeah." Micah smiled. "It's his fault."

She glared at him, playfully. "It's a good thing you're already hurt."

"Gee, thanks."

Luke kicked the door shut with his heel. "What did you pack, woman?"

She rushed over and took the lighter tote bag from him. "Food."

"You're an angel," Micah said.

"Did you get...?" She inspected the bags. "Oh, good. That heavy white bag on your shoulder is a cooler bag. All that is frozen meals. If there's not space in your freezer, we can put the largest container in the fridge to thaw for dinner tomorrow. That would be noodles and turkey."

Luke groaned. "I'm thawing that now even if there is room."

"I second that," Micah said.

"I can't believe you did this." Luke set the bags on the counter and pulled her in for another kiss. "How did I get so lucky?"

They stored the food quickly, Holly informing Luke what each container held. She intended to cook that weekend and leave the prepared food for when she returned north.

"Come upstairs," Luke said. "Show me where to put your suitcase."

"In her room, idiot."

"Shut up, little brother, or I'll take your potato chips away."

Holly shot Micah a glance, hoping he read "See?" on her face. Everyone treated him like a child. His shrug could have meant anything.

She followed Luke upstairs, sighing when he turned right. "I'm still in the guest room? After bringing food?"

"Nothing's going to happen with Micah on the couch."

"I see your point."

"And there's no hurry, anyway," Luke said. "We're building something lasting, right?"

"Right." She shrugged. "You're right. We'll get around to it."

He laughed and pushed her to the bed. She landed on her back with him over her. He stroked her hair back from her face and kissed her cheek. "I want to be with you, Holly." A kiss landed on the corner of her lips. "I think about making love to you all the time."

His mouth came down on hers, the urgency and heat leaving her in no doubt about his sincerity. His tongue relayed his intensity in a way mere words couldn't. Her heart pounded as his hands drove her wild, even knowing they wouldn't do more than kiss tonight. Anticipation made his caresses more exciting.

Abruptly, he sat up and pulled her with him. Luke took her hands in his. "While we've been apart, I've been thinking."

She smiled. "Oh-oh."

"I'm going to come to Chicago the minute that idiot can manage or I can find a home care nurse."

"I'd like that. Would it be possible to do it in the next few weeks?"

"I'd think so. If I have to care for him too long, I'll tip hot soup on him. He's getting on my nerves."

"You'll need a break. And it should be soon." She took a breath to launch in to what she had to say. Hoped he'd be happy about it.

"It'll be more than a break, Holly."

She frowned in confusion, feeling that she'd missed some conversation while plotting out her own speech. "It will?"

"Because I think we should live in Chicago."

Her heart stopped. *They* should live in Chicago? So, he was moving into her apartment and they'd be a couple? Just like that? Joy and disbelief warred within her. When she could find air, she gasped, "Are you serious?"

"You know what convinced me we should stay near your job?"

"No, what?" She felt like a parrot with a limited vocabulary. He was moving in with her. Santa must have heard her silent wish.

"Micah told me about your ideas to improve business for the Ivey Orchard. That's when I knew you're a natural at your job. Although Micah and I agreed, the Orchard's still not going to charge for hot chocolate."

She grinned. "One of the things I love this place is how it holds on to its traditions. That's one of your more admirable traits, too."

"Thanks. I think. My point was, if you can find possibilities in a small business like ours, marketing must be in your blood." He ran a finger down her cheek. "I can't take that away from you."

Since there was no whisky handy, she took a breath for courage. "Or."

"Or?"

"Or one might say I can do my job anywhere."

"True. I hadn't thought of it like that."

"Which is why I gave my two-week notice at work."

His face went blank.

"I want to be with you, Luke. I'm in love with you." His

stillness worried her. Maybe he wasn't ready. "I know it's a big step. I guess I should have talked to you first. I thought it would make things easier."

He yanked her into his arms, holding her tight.

Holly sagged with relief. Then she noticed his body shaking. "What?"

Sounds came from him. Turned into guffaws.

He drew back, laughing out loud. He calmed briefly, but a look at her face set him off again.

His hilarity became contagious, and she chuckled bewilderedly. "What's going on?"

"You...quit...your job." He wiped tears from his eyes, gaining control with a visible effort.

"You helped me believe in magic again, Luke. No job is worth the risk of losing you."

"That will never happen." He kissed her, sealing the vow. "The problem is, now we're both out of work."

She pulled back to look at him. "What do you mean?"

"I signed over my half of the Ivey Orchard and Christmas Tree Farm to Micah yesterday."

Her mouth dropped open. "You did what? Why?"

"To be with you. Don't worry about money," he said. "I have a tidy lump sum coming as soon as I can transport Micah to the bank. Then payments will come in each month until the purchase price is met."

"I wasn't thinking about the money. I'm just astonished."

"I'll find a job. I have mad skillz that will help me fit in in the city."

She smiled at his use of slang, loving him for trying to please her.

He cupped her face. "I can do a lot of things, Holly, but I can't do without you."

Tears formed in her eyes.

"I guess I'm doing this all backward, but will you marry me, Holly?"

She froze.

"I know it's quick. Probably--"

"Yes."

"--Too soon, but I--"

"Yes," she said more steadily.

"--Don't want to do without--" He stopped. "What did you say?"

She grinned. "I said yes. I'll marry you. Yes."

Luke whooped and kissed her. Then drew back and looked into her eyes. "You won't regret it, Holly."

"You won't either."

"I love you."

"I love you, too. I wish I could say I always have."

He shook his head. "It doesn't matter. We have each other now."

"We're so blessed. Fortunately, we were both free and open to love."

"I'm glad we'll be starting the new year together."

"The first of many," she said and drew him closer.

The love of her life had literally been the boy next door. She'd only needed some Christmas magic to realize it.

Thank you for reading Holly & Ivey.

If you missed the first Christmas in Stilton, *Santa Dear* is available in print and digital. Or head to Montana to "fall in Love in Little Tree." The first book is *The Wedding Rescue*.

Want a free short story in the Love in Little Tree world? Visit my website at megankellybooks.com and sign up for my newsletter. *A Risky Proposal* introduces you to Ryan, the hero of book four, *Coming Home*, but you can read it at any time.

If you enjoyed this book, I would appreciate you helping others find it.

* Recommend it. Please help other readers find this book by recommending it to friends, readers' groups, and discussion boards.

* Review it. Please use a few sentences to tell other readers why you liked this book by reviewing it at one of the following websites: a book seller site, BookBub or Goodreads.

About the Author

Megan Kelly fell in love with romance books in her teens and sees no end in sight. Thank goodness! Getting paid to follow her passion is the second-best job ever (next to being a mom/wife).

Megan lives with her husband and two children in the Midwest, where the weather has an imagination-—and sense of humor--of its own.

Please visit her website at megankellybooks.com and thanks for reading!!

Made in the USA
Monee, IL
09 June 2023